OATH

Nick Ryan

A World War 3 Technothriller Action Event

Copyright © 2024 Nicholas Ryan

The right of Nicholas Ryan to be identified as the author of this work has been asserted by him in accordance with the copyright, Designs and Patents Act 1988.

This is a work of fiction. Names, characters, places, and incidents either are the product of the author's imagination or are used fictitiously. Any resemblance to actual persons, living or dead, events, or locales is entirely coincidental.

All rights reserved. No part of this publication may be reproduced, stored in or introduced into a retrieval system, or transmitted, in any form, or by any other means (electronic, mechanical, photocopying, recording or otherwise) without the prior written permission of the author. Any person who does any unauthorized act in relation to this publication may be liable to criminal prosecution and civil claims for damages.

Dedication:
This book is dedicated to my fiancé, Ebony.
Every day, in every single way, she makes my world a better place.
-Nick.

About the Series:
The WW3 novels are a chillingly authentic collection of action-packed combat thrillers that envision a modern war where the world's superpowers battle on land, air and sea using today's military hardware.

Each title is a 50,000-word stand-alone adventure that forms part of an ever-expanding series.

Website: https://www.worldwar3timeline.com

Other titles in the collection:
- 'Charge to Battle'
- 'Enemy in Sight'
- 'Viper Mission'
- 'Fort Suicide'
- 'The Killing Ground'
- 'Search and Destroy'
- 'Airborne Assault'
- 'Defiant to the Death'
- 'A Time for Heroes'
- 'Oath of Honor'

The Invasion of China

After several weeks of protracted military build-up along the North Korean border, the American-led 'Coalition of Freedom' forces finally commenced their ground war into China during the first days of August. The invasion was preceded by a wave of mass artillery bombardments that turned enemy installations, buildings, highways and fortifications into rubble.

In the aftermath of the terrible barrage, allied forces moved confidently from their assembly points within occupied North Korea, planning to strike across the Yalu River in three great waves.

Freedom Army A's objective was to drive north from the city of Sinuiju to attempt to seize the important Chinese port city of Dandong.

Freedom Army B's objective was to push north from Manp'o towards the city of Tonghua, located seventy kilometers over the disputed border.

Freedom Army C's objective was to cross the Yalu River from bases around the city of Samjiyon, near Mount Paektu, intending to seize a major inland road network and intersection that would prevent the Chinese from counter-attacking the flanks of the two main invading armies.

The Chinese forces arrayed along the border were well prepared in defensive positions. For weeks prior to the commencement of hostilities, the enemy had been rushing troops into the disputed region, working around the clock to fortify artillery emplacements and evacuating civilians.

For the American assault troops that would constitute the iron fist of the initial attack, there would be no element of surprise to aid them. The fight for China would be a violent clash of brute force: a war of shock and awe.

The U.S. ground forces who fought their way across the Yalu in the early frantic hours of G-Day were supported by jet fighters and heavy bombers who flew hundreds of sorties from land bases across the Korean Peninsula.

Preliminary allied assessments from intelligence satellites along the Chinese border were encouraging. Coalition command reported that after just a few hours of fierce fighting, soldiers from Freedom Army B and light armored vehicles attached to Freedom Army C had made successful crossings of the Yalu and had established positions on Chinese soil. Most importantly, the troops assaulting Dandong city over a network of makeshift bridges had established a toe-hold on the northern bank of the river and were digging in.

But success quickly turned to stalemate, and within days the three-pronged assault north had begun to stall.

The Chinese divisions defending the city of Dandong launched a massive counter-attack, trying to drive the Americans back into the river.

Allied Command understood that the few thousand men clinging to the northern riverbank suburbs of Dandong had to be reinforced quickly. A second wave of men were sent forward; battle-hardened veteran units who had campaigned their way through North Korea.

The American commanders on the front lines of the fight were given a grim, chilling ultimatum.

Dandong must fall quickly, or else the entire invasion of China would be put in jeopardy.

ZHENXING DISTRICT, DANDONG CITY CHINA

Chapter 1:

Medics were pulling charred bodies from the nearby ruins of a destroyed M1126 Stryker as the men from Alpha Company, 3rd Battalion, 15th Infantry Regiment assembled in the vehicle park on the southern side of the river and prepared to file onto the bailey bridge that traversed the Yalu into China.

Two F-16's flashed across the sullen sky, their afterburners lit, and the air seemed to shake and tremble as the infantrymen joined the endless line of troops and trucks shunting northwards. Dawn came on swiftly, revealing a bleak cloud-filled horizon, heavy with imminent rain and crackling with fraught tension.

Three Divisional MPs, tasked with coordinating the movement of units across the choke-point, approached the men of Alpha Company. The female corporal in command brusquely ordered the troops onto the bridge with no-nonsense authority.

"Go now! Move it, move it."

The company had been ordered by Brigade to act as security for logistical and maintenance units, leaving the unit tasked out from the rest of their battalion during the previous day's calamitous river crossing. The men were eager to rejoin their unit and take the fight to the enemy. Throughout the fraught night, radio comms from HQ had reported that 3rd Battalion had taken up positions in buildings two miles north of the riverbank. For Alpha Company, reaching their comrades before the Chinese launched another counter-attack had become a race against time.

Captain Buck 'Razor' Gillette had spent the past two months on the Chinese border and was acutely aware of the region's fickle weather patterns. He cast a wary eye skyward, then led his men forward, peering ahead at the devastated hellish landscape the company were marching towards.

The stench of rotting flesh, mingled with diesel fumes and choking clouds of smoke from burning buildings, coated the back of Gillette's throat.

The evidence of the previous day's bloody fighting was everywhere Gillette looked. The cityscape of Dandong had been obliterated by allied artillery fire and air strikes, leaving the skyline a ruinous mess of twisted carnage beneath a sooty black haze of drifting ash. The rubble-strewn streets were littered with the burned-out hulks of dozens of destroyed tanks and the river was choked with mutilated corpses that floated downstream on the sluggish current or washed up as flotsam along the riverbank.

"Speed it up, Mario," Gillette growled. "There's a shit-storm of pain heading our way. I can feel it in my guts. I want our boys off this damned bailey bridge and into cover before the Chinese open fire."

Lieutenant Mario Tonneguzzi, Alpha company's Executive Officer, nodded dutifully.

"Roger that, boss. I'll go forward and see what the hold-up is."

The company's troops were heavily laden with weapons, ammunition, and kit, and the makeshift bridge was choked with infantry and a column of HEMTT 'Dragon Wagon' trucks, that were all funneling north towards the ruined outskirts of Dandong city. The bailey bridge was just one of several that spanned the Yalu. Five hundred yards further downstream stretched a pair of massive float ribbon bridges, sagging beneath the weight of M1 Abrams tanks and M2 Bradley fighting vehicles, and two more ribbon bridges lay another mile further to the west. All the bridges had been assembled overnight by men from the 74th MRBC, 62nd Engineer Battalion, who were still hard at work on the south side of the river, the revving roar of their heavy equipment adding to the wall of noise that was so overwhelmingly loud it seemed to drown out even the muted mind-numbing crump of distant allied artillery fire.

Gillette turned his attention back to his troops as the men continued to file past him. They were mud-spattered and haggard, unshaven and exhausted, but they all marched with the assured swagger of soldiers who had stared down death and emerged triumphant in the face of their fears. They grinned laconically at their captain as they trooped by, and Gillette grinned back. A sergeant from 3rd Platoon held out a crumpled pack of cigarettes. Gillette shook his head.

They were battle-toughened veterans of the bloody fight for Seoul and a proud part of the 3rd Division, based out of Fort Stewart, Georgia. Though most of the Division were mechanized troops, the men of 3rd Battalion, 2nd Brigade were light infantry. They were proud, skilled warriors, and Captain Buck Gillette, a hard-as-nails Ranger qualified officer, felt privileged to lead them into battle.

A sudden commotion of noise made Gillette look up quickly. From somewhere beyond the press of milling soldiers and idling heavy trucks at the north end of the bridge, Gillette heard the sudden unmistakable rattle of Chinese machine gun fire. The drumming roar seemed to echo on the air, not close enough to cause panic, but near enough for the infantry captain to look up with a flash of urgent tension.

Mario Tonneguzzi reappeared, frazzled, his face working with agitation.

"Whose firing?" Gillette demanded.

"Apparently there's a Chinese heavy machine gun in a destroyed building about two clicks to the north."

"Is that the reason for the hold up?" Gillette frowned.

"No," the XO shook his head. "One of the HEMTT's at the front of the column has broken down. Headquarters is waiting for a recovery vehicle to haul it to the side of the road."

Gillette winced, then swore his frustration. It was always the insignificant unforeseen things that caused crisis. "How long?"

Tonneguzzi shrugged. Like the rest of the men in the company, the XO's uniform was shabby and mud-stained, his face dark with unshaven stubble. "Ten minutes. Maybe fifteen."

"Shit. If we don't get off this bridge soon, we're going to get caught by a storm of enemy artillery. Any minute now the Chinese are going to rain a fury of righteous wrath down on us."

"Maybe the enemy retreated last night," the XO offered, more in hope than conviction. "Maybe they've pulled back beyond the city's outskirts."

Gillette shook his head. "Take a look around you, Mario. The Chinese kicked our ass yesterday. They're not going anywhere. They're going to fight it out. Right now, I reckon they're dug in amongst the ruins, just waiting for us to stumble across their sights. This city will become another god-damned Stalingrad if we don't seize the upper hand quickly."

Two more Air Force F-16 Vipers went racing northwards, flying low, their great engines howling. Fifteen seconds later a cluster of bomb-ravaged apartment blocks north of the bridge erupted into fireballs of flame and boiling smoke. Gillette stood at the bailey's steel railing and watched the explosions bloom high into the sky. One of the buildings became engulfed in flames. Another apartment block fell crumbling to the ground amidst a massive cloud of smoke and dust.

In the wake of the twin explosions, the world seemed to fall eerily silent for a fateful heartbeat – and then the Chinese artillery suddenly opened fire and drowned out everything with roaring mindless fury.

"Christ!" Gillette swore and intuitively sank to his haunches, one hand clamping his helmet tight to his head. Tonneguzzi gaped in dismay, then cringed for cover. The Yalu River suddenly erupted into a tsunami of white water and the bridge beneath their feet began to heave and buck like a wild horse. The air filled with the whistling whine of incoming shells and the river turned into a seething cauldron.

"Get the men off this bridge, Mario!" Gillette had to bellow to make himself heard above the obscene scream of the barrage as shells rained down all around them. "Go! Go! Go!"

The XO ran forward, doubled over, jinking as the air filled with shrapnel. A man from 2nd Platoon was killed, struck in the back of the head, his helmet thrown spinning into the air in a cloud of bright blood.

Gillette forced himself to his feet and ran after his XO, weaving as shards of burning metal whistled and cracked about his ears. Behind him, an engineer cried out in agony and Gillette heard him fall screaming. But he did not stop, nor look around. His priority was to get to the end of the bridge and force a way through the trucks so his troops could reach safety.

He caught up to his XO and the two men ran on together. A Chinese artillery round landed in the river just fifty yards to their right and heaved a bright cascade of rushing water over the bridge, rocking the tethered spans so that the steel beneath their feet buckled and flexed. Mario Tonneguzzi fell sprawling to the ground and Gillette stooped and hefted the other man back to his feet without seeming to break stride. Then suddenly, incredibly, they were at the north end of the bridge and forcing their way, shouting and punching to clear a path.

"Alpha Company! Alpha Company!" Gillette clenched his fist and pumped it into the air. "Get off the bridge! Move! Move!"

The road beyond the riverbank had been cratered and gouged by twenty-four hours of relentless artillery fire and Gillette steered his men towards the shallow cover, pushing and shoving them, swearing and yelling until his voice rasped painfully in his throat and his senses became swamped by the cacophony of incoming explosions. One of the heavy HEMTT's at the front of the stalled column took a direct hit from a Chinese mortar shell and was torn open like a wet paper bag. The truck burst into drumming flames and a column of thick oily smoke billowed into the dawn sky while the trapped driver in the truck's cab screamed and beat at the fire with his bare hands until he was incinerated. The sickly-sweet stench of the man's roasting flesh drifted like a gagging pall on the air.

Mario Tonneguzzi threw himself into a shell crater and Gillette dived after the XO, both men gasping and heaving for breath. Gillette turned and peered back over his shoulder. The bailey bridge was swarming with troops from other units, crowded into a bottleneck between the stalled HEMTTs. Another Chinese artillery shell exploded in the river, landing so close to the bridge that several support pontoons were blown apart and the center span suddenly sagged alarmingly. The soldiers still ensnared on the bridge lurched for handholds to keep their balance, then devolved into a struggling cursing rabble, infected with wild panic.

Gillette could only watch on in horror and curse his bitter frustration.

"The bridge is going to collapse," he croaked, appalled. "Every one of those poor bastards will be killed."

Some of the desperate soldiers trapped on the bridge sensed death's imminent embrace and threw themselves into the heaving brown water of the Yalu. Others turned and tried to retreat across the creaking steel spans, cursing and flailing in sheer terror.

Chinese troops concealed in the bomb-shattered buildings that lined the riverbank suddenly opened fire and the bridge became an abattoir; a bloody charnel house of dead and dying. The hail of bullets cut a swathe through the milling masses of American soldiers and the steel bridge spans turned red with blood. Amongst the screams of fear and agony, muted voices rose, trying to rally the trapped.

"We've walked into an ambush! Return fire!"

"Get off the bridge!"

"For God's sake, why isn't our arty firing smoke?"

"Jesus Christ! What happened to our fighter cover?"

Some of the dead were scythed down where they stood. Others were hurled, bleeding, into the churning water. One man was struck low in the guts and doubled over, moaning, clutching at himself while blood spurted through his fingers. The screams of the dying gradually faded into incoherent pitiful groans because there was no one left standing to kill.

Then the Chinese artillery found its range and a shell landed flush in the center of the bridge. The fiery explosion tore the bailey in half and flung bodies and twisted steel cartwheeling high into the air.

Buck Gillette watched on in helpless horror until a shroud of black smoke enveloped the nightmare.

The new day – that just moments before had promised swift and savage vengeance against the enemy – had suddenly spiraled into disaster.

And then things got even worse.

*

The leaden sky overhead filled with a fresh storm of artillery fire and the ruined city blocks north of the river became suddenly blanketed in thick clouds of grey haze. The allied artillery had finally begun firing smoke missions on their pre-registered targets throughout the city.

Too late.

The blanket of smoke had been intended to cover the advancing American infantry as they pushed towards the heart of Dandong. Now it was sheltering the few thousand men and tanks who had been stranded along the riverbank.

"We're cut off," Mario Tonneguzzi had seen the bailey bridge collapse into the Yalu. "The nearest bridge back across the river is five hundred yards away – if it's still standing."

Gillette rose onto his haunches and peered carefully above the lip of the crater. The smoke reduced visibility to just a few dozen yards, but he saw the rest of the company spread out around him, sheltering in similar craters. Intuitively, the troops had arrayed themselves in a makeshift defensive perimeter around the bridgehead. Some of the men were on their knees, head and shoulders raised above ground level and anxiously covering the fields of fire directly ahead of their positions, searching the swirling veil of smoke for threats. Others lay in cover with their backs against the gouged earth, hastily drinking water or dressing flesh wounds.

Gillette cocked his ear and frowned. From somewhere within the grey veil, and above the sound of exploding artillery shells, he could hear the unmistakable rumble of tank engines. But whether they were Abrams tanks or Chinese tanks, he could not be sure.

He ducked back down into cover and withered Mario Tonneguzzi with a resolute glare and an arrogant thrust of his chin. "We're Alpha Company. We don't run from a god-damned fight, no matter the odds," he said. "We crossed that bridge with orders to report to Battalion HQ and that's exactly what we're going to do."

The rest of the Battalion were dug in and defending positions somewhere north of Alpha company's location and reaching them was as much a matter of pride as duty for Captain Buck Gillette.

Sporadic gunfire broke out, coming from destroyed buildings along the riverbank. Gillette turned to his XO; his decision made.

He snatched the radio from his RTO (Radio Telephone Operator) and held the handset out to Tonneguzzi. "Get on comms to Lieutenant Colonel Reilly. Find out where HQ is and give him a SITREP. Tell him we're on our way to his location. Then get on the company net and inform the platoon leaders. We're moving forward in fifteen minutes, come hell or high water."

"Where are you going?"

"I'm going to check on the men."

Gillette braced himself beneath the lip of the crater, took a single deep breath and then bounded to his feet, running doubled over. He felt the wind of a stray bullet blow hot against his cheek. The sound of small arms fire intensified all around him. He took a dozen long strides and threw himself into another nearby crater.

There were a handful of men slumped down in the shallow pit, covered in drifting dust and ash. Gillette glanced about himself quickly. During the chaotic scramble off the bridge, everyone in the company had simply flung themselves into the nearest available cover. Gillette recognized the lieutenant leading the company's Fire Support Team. The FIST lieutenant was a grim-faced, taciturn New Yorker named Geyer who seemed more pissed-off than rattled.

"Where's the rest of your team?" Gillette got eye contact with the other man. Lieutenant Geyer hawked a wad of bloody phlegm into the dirt and shook his head. "Fucked if I know, sir," he said bitterly. "I think Harrigan is dead. The rest of my team got spread out amongst the company when the shit hit the fan."

Gillette grunted. He glanced around at the rest of the men sheltering about him. They were grimy with dirt and sweat, but their eyes, when he looked into their faces, were steady. They'd been through worse and survived.

"We're moving out in fifteen minutes," Gillette declared.

"We're retreating back across the river, sir?" a man on the far side of the crater asked.

"Hell no," Gillette growled. "The rest of the Battalion is somewhere north of here, maybe just a click or two away. We're going to rejoin with them because we're the best goddamned company in the Division and they need our support to win this fight. Hooah!"

"Hooah!" the men shouted back.

*

Mario Tonneguzzi was waiting for Gillette when he returned a handful of minutes later, covered in dirt and sweat. The crump of exploding Chinese mortar and artillery rounds echoed around the nearby bomb-damaged buildings, seeming to be drawing closer.

"How are the men?" the XO asked.

"Spread out all across the damned riverbank," Gillette scowled and sucked in a heaving breath. "Three confirmed dead for sure, but there might be more. A dozen wounded, but they can all fight on. Where is Reilly?"

Tonneguzzi pulled a map from his breast pocket and unfolded it. He tapped a point with the tip of his finger and Gillette peered.

"Battalion HQ is a mile-and-a-half north northwest of us," the XO creased the map with his thumbnail. "As far as I can figure, the fastest route is to follow this road north until we reach an intersection. The rest of the way will be through backstreets and alleys. These apartment buildings," Tonneguzzi indicated a cluster of small shapes on the map arranged in an echelon, flanked by a narrow strip of green, "are being secured by Bravo and Charlie companies. Apparently, their position overlooks a parking lot, a cluster of low-rise residential blocks, and some kind of ornamental public garden space."

Gillette grunted. "And the Chinese? Where are they?"

The XO looked up sharply and made a ghoulish face. "The Chinese are everywhere we ain't," the XO said gravely.

It was a salient point. After more than twenty-four hours of fighting, the allies were still hemmed in to a strip of Dandong's riverbank that measured just a couple of miles deep and five miles wide. Within that small space were several thousand men and several hundred tanks – but the allies would need a much greater force if they were ever to mount a concerted attack towards the heart of the sprawling Chinese metropolis. Every intersection, every tall building, every piece of elevated terrain would be defended, and each inch of ground the allies won would have to be paid for with blood. Chinese artillery, massed in batteries to the north and northeast of the city's outskirts, would have every significant landmark and road junction within a fifteen-mile radius of the river pre-registered for fire missions. Every enemy held vantage point would be manned by observers. As soon as the Americans tried to launch an attack, they would come under immediate savage fire.

But for the allies to do nothing other than defend the ground they had gained was to die a slow death of attrition; pounded into dust by a relentless barrage of Chinese HE.

The sudden sound of jet fighters directly overhead brought Gillette's head snapping up. The echo of the roaring engines seemed to reverberate off the low cloud cover. He squinted his eyes, peered forty-five degrees ahead of where the sound seemed to be coming from in the sky, and after a heartbeat he noticed three delta-winged Chinese fighters. They were approaching from the north, flying beneath the clouds. He flicked a questioning glance at Tonneguzzi.

"They look like J-10 Firebirds," the XO opined. He was the company's resident expert on military aircraft and Gillette didn't for a moment doubt the man's assessment. "Multi-role fighters. They might be trying to bomb the ribbon bridges."

Gillette watched the sleek black shapes race closer, growing in size by the second, flying wing-tip to wing-tip. Then suddenly the right-hand fighter burst into a brilliant billowing fireball of flames and went cartwheeling across the sky.

"Christ!" Gillette gasped.

"Vipers!" the XO pointed jubilantly an instant later as two F-16 fighters burst through the cloud cover like birds of prey, their M61 Vulcan Gattling-style rotary cannons blazing.

The remaining two Chinese J-10's broke apart, banking left and right and climbing, desperate to gain altitude. The Vipers were too quick, too nimble. Another J-10 was hit, spinning end over end as it blew apart. The stricken fighter crashed behind a distant office block in a black pall of oily smoke.

The last J-10 disappeared above the clouds with the two Vipers hot on its tail. Gillette had seen enough. He scrambled up the side of the crater.

"Come on!" he roared and waved his hand, urging the men around him to break cover. "Follow me! Alpha Company, on me!"

Gillette started running and from the cratered earth the men of Alpha Company rose out of their ditches and ran after him. The ground was rubble-strewn and littered with broken glass, and ahead of them a destroyed Stryker sagged, a gaping black hole torn through the side of the vehicle, its tires still smoldering, the ground grey with ash and two dead bodies in the dirt nearby. Gillette reached the burnt-out ICV and quickly scanned the route ahead. A wide road ran north from the riverbank; an avenue that stretched away into the smoke-veiled distance. The buildings on both sides of the blacktop had been ravaged by allied artillery so that some of the tall office blocks had collapsed completely while others stood, leaning precariously, their empty windows blackened, the sidewalks heaped with great chunks of rubble and dead, mangled corpses. The road was scorched and potholed, and small fires still burned in some of the derelict buildings. In places, the road ahead was choked with rubble and the twisted ruins of overturned cars and burned-out tanks.

Gillette eyed the scorched façades of the closest buildings with dread and fatalistic resolve. The only way to reach Battalion HQ was to run the gauntlet. A slimy reptile of fear twisted in the pit of his guts. There would be Chinese troops amongst the ruins, he knew for sure, and a hundred American infantrymen storming down the street would prove an irresistible target. He imagined a cross-fire of enemy machine guns scything through his troops, cutting them down like wheat, and balked.

It was a death trap. Gillette swore softly, then cast about desperately for an alternative route, but amidst the chaos of incoming enemy artillery fire he could see nothing but explosions and smoke.

He crouched behind a mound of fallen bricks and glanced over his shoulder. Tonneguzzi was right behind him and so was his RTO.

"Tell the men to disperse into cover as best they can until I give the order to advance. Then find Sergeant Fletcher. I want the M240s and a couple of Javelin teams here, pronto!" he told his XO, then searched the press of grime and sweat-stained faces for his FIST lieutenant.

"Geyer! Get on the radio to our arty. I want smoke between here and the end of this avenue, ASAP!"

Lieutenant Geyer reached for his radio and cut into the artillery frequency.

"Stepbrother Six this is Ugly Duckling Four requesting smoke at TRP nine. Over."

The radio crackled in Geyer's ear for a dozen thumping heartbeats and then a disconnected voice broke the fraught silence.

"Ugly Duckling Four this is Stepbrother Six. Smoke at TRP nine. Out."

The artillery pieces tasked to support Alpha Company were four M777A2 155mm howitzers from the 2nd Field Artillery Regiment, positioned on a rise of ground four kilometers south of the Yalu River.

After the FCO confirmed Geyer's request, several more tense seconds passed before Geyer received the confirmation transmission.

"Shot over."

"Shot out," the lieutenant acknowledged and then flicked Gillette a calm, competent glance while waiting for the 'splash' call.

Tonneguzzi brought the heavy weapons teams forward. The men crouched close to Gillette, burdened by the awkward weight of their weapons, their faces tight with tension.

Gillette pointed across the expanse of wide-open road and then addressed each man, his face pressed close, his voice urgent. "I want covering fire from an M240 and a Javelin amongst that pile of rubble," he indicated the collapsed ruin of a shopfront almost directly opposite from where he crouched. "And I want another M240 and Javelin on the first floor of that building," he pointed again at a low-rise office block. "If anything moves on this street or comes trundling through the smoke cover, I want it blown to fucking bite-sized pieces. Understand?"

The team members nodded, somber and silent, then moved out, crouched low, while a half-dozen men armed with M4s covered them.

The first smoke rounds fell in the middle of the avenue even before the Javelin and machine gun teams were in place. Gillette heard the low whine of the incoming shells as they plunged down out of the clouds and a moment later the view ahead was blanketed in a wall of white swirling smoke. He waited impatiently for a count of ten seconds, then sprang from cover and waved men forward.

"First platoon, take the lead. Go! Go! Take up covering positions to secure the intersection at the far end of the street."

The sergeant leading 1st Platoon barked at his men, then charged towards the smoke. His troops ran after him, each individual swerving and jinking, pausing to take up covering positions, then dashing forward again, leapfrogging each other until they became swallowed up by the thick pall of haze.

Gillette let out a great exhalation of breath he hadn't realized had been jammed in his throat. He waited, tensed and dread-filled for the snarl of an enemy machine gun or the whip-crack of a Chinese sniper rifle – but the avenue remained eerily silent.

"First platoon are on comms. They've reached the intersection and are taking up covering positions," the RTO reported.

Gillette nodded, relieved. "Alpha Company, go!" he waved the rest of the men forward.

The rest of the company broke from cover like Olympic sprinters, each man with their own personal terror snapping at their heels. Gillette led the rush into the shroud of smoke. Then suddenly the sound of rifle fire cut through the tension and the man beside Gillette went down, struck in the head. The impact bludgeoned the soldier sideways, his rifle spinning from his hands, screeching with pain and astonishment as he collapsed to the blacktop.

"Medic!" Gillette barked, then ran on, elbows pumping and his breath sawing across his throat as the smoke around him seemed to thicken until he could barely see a few paces in front of him. Another shot whip-sawed from somewhere high and to his left. Then a Chinese machine gun opened fire, thrashing the air with chattering death, shooting blindly into the smoke but getting hits. Bullets twitched holes in the smoke and ricocheted off nearby rubble. Gillette flinched instinctively but ran on. Behind him he could hear the pounding beat of his men's boots thundering across the blacktop and the clinks and rattles of their equipment.

The Chinese machine gun fired again and a voice amongst the smoke screamed in strangled agony.

"Christ!" Gillette gritted his teeth, snarling bitter frustration. He paused and let a dozen men run past him. "Move! Faster! Faster!" he urged them to greater effort. More Chinese machine gun fire shredded the smoke, tearing gouges out of the blacktop and cracking viciously through the air. Gillette saw a corporal from 2nd Platoon punched to the ground and he stared, aghast.

The man lay with his arms flung wide, the jaw and the right side of his face blown away, teeth and gruesome shards of white bone protruding through the bloody pulp. The man's body twitched in a paroxysm of heaving spasms, his pale clawed hands plucking feebly at the dirt.

A second man ran through a fusillade of stray enemy bullets and was spun in a jerky grotesque circle, his arms flailing, his head wrenched back until his legs collapsed beneath him and he fell flapping to the ground in a gushing wash of bright blood.

"Medic!" Gillette bellowed.

The roar of an M240 growled back in spiteful counter-fire and a split-second later an explosion shook the ground and brought a hail of tumbling debris falling to the ground. Gillette recognized the retort of a Javelin and he snarled savage satisfaction, then ran on until the swirling banks of cloud thinned and suddenly the eerie silhouettes of three destroyed Chinese tanks ghosted into sight. They were old Type-96's, splayed across the intersection. One of the Chinese tanks sagged on broken tracks, its turret upended, and the hull scorched black. The other two MBT's were still intact, but their steel frontal armor was punched through with holes, their turrets traversed backwards, their barrels drooped low. The turret hatch of one of the tanks was flung open and the body of a dead Chinese tank officer lay slumped, half hanging out of the opening. Some of the men from 1st Platoon were using the destroyed tank hulks for cover, kneeling or lying prone in the carnage of charred, blackened debris that littered the tarmac.

Gillette got eye contact with 1st Platoon's sergeant who nodded in acknowledgment, and then he noticed a handful of battle-haggard soldiers whose faces he didn't immediately recognize. The officer leading the men sauntered forward confidently and acknowledged Gillette. He was young, with haunted eyes that were sunk deep into their sockets.

"Welcome to hell, sir," the lieutenant said grimly. "Lieutenant Colonel Reilly is waiting for you. Me and my men are here to escort your boys to Battalion HQ."

Chapter 2:

Battalion HQ was a shell-ravaged low-rise apartment building with an old grocery store on the ground floor, beneath five stories of residential accommodation. The building had been devastated by allied artillery fire in the days leading up to the ground attack and seemed on the verge of collapse. The street at both ends was blocked by twisted steel and a rubble of bricks. As Alpha Company approached the site, Gillette noticed three grime-coated Oshkosh M-ATV's parked beneath the shelter of a sagging brick wall.

"The Lieutenant Colonel is waiting for you through that door, sir," the young officer who had commanded the detachment of escorts pointed. "I'll make sure your men get some chow, something to drink, and medical attention. Food and water we've got aplenty, but I can't guarantee much rest. The Chinese artillery has been darn restless in this sector. It's likely to get rowdy."

Gillette nodded, then glanced at Tonneguzzi. The two men strode through a sandbag-protected door into a gloomy office at the rear of the grocery store.

It was a large space that had once been the shop's stock room. The shelves that lined the walls were heaped with discarded combat gear, small arms ammunition and webbing belts slung with kit. Radio equipment had been piled high on two long tables and a map of Dandong city taped over a cracked window, blocking out the only light source. Gillette stood still for a long moment and let his eyes adjust to the sudden gloom.

In the far corner, Lieutenant Colonel John Reilly sat in a rickety chair behind a small steel office desk. He ran a calm, appraising eye over Gillette's sweat and blood-spattered uniform, then flicked a glance at Tonneguzzi.

"I heard from Brigade about the river crossing," Reilly said from behind a desk littered with paperwork. "Heard it was bad."

Gillette nodded. "The Chinese must have had us under observation the entire time," Gillette confirmed. "Once a few thousand men were onto the northern bank, they pounded the bridges with artillery fire. We were the last unit safely across. The bailey took a direct hit, but some of the floating bridges the heavy armor used were still standing last time I looked. Sir."

Reilly grunted. He was a small-framed man in his forties with a buzz-cut of greying hair and a weather-lined face, wearing combat fatigues that seemed too large for his slight physique. But despite the man's unremarkable stature, his eyes were steely-grey and steady. They were the eyes of an experienced warrior who had seen more than his share of horror. He had served on the front lines in the Middle East and Syria. He flashed Gillette a tight wintry smile devoid of any trace of humor.

"The Chinese are fucking with us," Reilly declared. "They're drip-feeding our boys to their guns, and until we can force a major and sustained crossing, those of us stranded on the north bank of the Yalu are vulnerable. The Chinese probably have close to a hundred thousand men spread throughout this city. If they decide to go on the offensive..." his voice trailed off, the menace implicit.

For a long moment the Lieutenant Colonel seemed lost in his own dark thoughts, and then his head snapped up suddenly, his eyes slamming back into focus. "You said Alpha Company was the last unit safely across the bridge?"

"Yes, sir."

"Wounded?"

"A handful."

"Dead?"

"Three crossing the Yalu. At least three more since. We were ambushed by an enemy machine gun enroute from the riverbank."

Reilly made a pained face, then nodded. Casualties were an unavoidable consequence of war. He sighed and seemed to shake off the bad news because what lay ahead seemed eminently worse.

"One rogue enemy machine gun in a ruined building is going to be the least of your problems, captain. We're in the eye of a storm here. This is the hottest sector in the fiercest fight that the war in Asia is likely to see," he turned then and went to the map of Dandong city, a brusque business-like snap in his step. He described a small circle with his finger.

"Our ground forces are holding this small sector of Zhenxing District, north of the river. Our armor that has made it across the Yalu is concentrating to the east of us throughout Yianbao District, but the tanks remain isolated in pockets and haven't been yet able to link up into an effective fighting force. Nor have they been able to break through to our position which means – for the moment at least – we are cut-off and unsupported."

The news was confirmation of a dire situation, not a surprise to either Gillette or Tonneguzzi. The first twenty-four hours of the ground attack into China had not gone according to allied plans and now high command was scrambling to remedy the situation by forcing more men across the river.

The hawks within the Coalition of Freedom's halls of power had predicted that the enemy troops defending Dandong would be overwhelmed swiftly by the free world's massed military might and the city would fall with little resistance.

The men on the ground who would be called upon to win the victory knew better. Nobody ever accused the Chinese of being stupid. Their troops were well-drilled and disciplined. Their equipment was inferior, but that weakness was made up for by sheer quantity; the PLA Ground Force numbered almost a million men, augmented by another half-million men in reserve and serving in paramilitary units; it was a massive army, supplemented by thousands of tanks and batteries of artillery – all stitched together by a sophisticated communications system, a serviceable road infrastructure – and a secret sprawling network of subterranean tunnels.

It was the tunnels that worried Gillette the most. During the build-up to the outbreak of war, he and the rest of the Division's leaders had been briefed by members of the Army's Asymmetric Warfare Group about the prospect of fighting underground as they battled through North Korea and into China. One of the Army's most recent manuals on the subject suggested that the North Koreans could accommodate the transfer of thirty thousand heavily armed troops per hour through their tunnel networks, and Gillette had no doubts the Chinese had built an equally sophisticated subterranean network.

Perhaps there were even enemy tunnels right beneath where he stood.

The unsettling thought sent a clammy chill running down his spine, and rather than dwell on the disturbing concern, he interrupted the Lieutenant Colonel in the midst of his briefing.

"What's our role, sir?"

Lieutenant Colonel Reilly turned sharply from the map. But instead of speaking he strode from the room, his footsteps echoing hollowly through the empty cavernous expanse of the derelict grocery store. Part of the ceiling had collapsed in a pile of plaster and errant power cables dangled down from the roof like jungle vines. Gillette and Tonneguzzi exchanged a puzzled glance, then followed the senior officer.

"There," Reilly pointed out through the store's cracked glass shopfront. "See those two apartment buildings on the far side of the ornamental park? Bravo Company has occupied the southern building and Charlie Company holds the one to the north. Your task is to relieve Charlie Company."

Gillette seemed disappointed. "Is that all, sir?"

"It's enough," Reilly growled a warning and spent a long moment scrutinizing Captain Buck Gillette's face before he spoke again. Though his expression did not change, the man's voice hardened.

"Those two buildings mark the perimeter, gentlemen," his eyes flicked from Gillette to Tonneguzzi. "Everything past those buildings as far as you can see is enemy territory."

"Have the Chinese attacked, sir?" the XO asked.

"No," the Lieutenant Colonel shook his head like a small spaniel shaking itself dry after a bath. "But they will. It's just a matter of time. The enemy know they have us completely outnumbered. They know we're isolated and vulnerable. An attack is inevitable – but until that moment, your posture is to remain completely defensive," he turned back to Gillette and said meaningfully, "Under no circumstances are you to provoke the enemy. Every minute the Chinese delay their assault is an extra minute that we have to get more men and armor across the river."

"I understand," Gillette nodded, his discontent apparent.

"I hope you do," Reilly warned. "You have a reputation, Captain Gillette; a not altogether desirable one. A lot of senior officers on staff think you're arrogant, and a little too assured of your own abilities. You would do well not to let your ego get in the way of your duty."

Gillette said nothing.

*

The rally point for Alpha Company was a cratered parking lot behind the grocery store.

Gillette and Tonneguzzi were chowing down with their men when a senior officer appeared from inside the building. Gillette rose to his feet.

Battalion XO, Major Guy Yee, thrust out his hand towards Gillette and smiled.

"Good to see you in one piece, Razor. I'm glad you and your boys got off that bridge before the Chinese destroyed it."

The two officers shook hands, then sauntered casually away from the resting men until they were standing close to the battalion's parked Oshkosh M-ATV's. From where they stood both men had a view across the ravaged remains of the ornamental gardens and parkland to the apartment buildings 3rd Battalion were defending.

"The boss has asked me to take you forward and arrange the relief-in-place," Major Yee explained. The two men knew each other well and the major was a friendly, informal officer with the soft-spoken manner of a country preacher. The troops had nicknamed him 'Daddy Yee'.

"Charlie Company have been standing their post for over twenty-four hours. They're going to appreciate time off the line."

"Has there been any activity from the enemy?" Gillette probed.

Major Yee shrugged dismissively. "Once in a while the Chinese open fire just to keep our boys on edge and alert," he said. "No artillery. No concerted ground attacks – just sporadic machine gun fire and flares. They're using H and I to fuck with our morale."

"So, the bastards taunting us?" Gillette asked. 'H and I' was military shorthand for harassment and interdiction fire – a tactic that was as old as warfare itself.

"Yes. They know we're isolated. They're just biding their time," the senior officer said – then fell ominously silent.

Gillette grunted. The air was thick with the stench of oily smoke and a gentle breeze off the river carried with it a haze of drifting dust. The storm clouds overhead had begun to break apart revealing patches of blue mid-morning sky. Major Yee scratched at unshaven stubble then yawned. His eyes were red-rimmed and glassy with fatigue. Gillette doubted anyone in the unit had slept much in the past day.

The two officers strolled back towards the waiting company, taking care to appear blithely unworried, aware that the men would be watching them for signs of tension or despondency. Despite the grim situation, it was important the senior commanders appeared supremely assured at all times.

Gillette gestured to Tonneguzzi. "Get the men on their feet and ready, XO. We're moving forward to the front line."

The tragedy of the ruined ornamental Chinese gardens was lost on the men of Alpha Company as they trudged forward under the burdens of their combat kit, weapons and bulky equipment. Just two days ago this strip of grassy nature had been in full bloom; the intricate garden beds bursting with vibrant flowering color and the trees burgeoning with a myriad of singing birdlife. Now the parkland precinct was a post-apocalyptic wasteland of brown churned earth, broken rock and charred ruin. The trees had been stripped bare of their leaves by incessant allied artillery barrages and the flower beds destroyed. Because of its close proximity to the planned allied army's river crossings, this sector of Zhenxing District had been one of the hardest hit by Coalition bombardments in the lead up to G-Day.

Major Yee led the way with Gillette at his side, navigating a meandering course through the ruined chaos with the rest of the company following in loose order. When they reached the ground floor of the northernmost apartment complex, two men from Charlie Company were waiting by the broken ruins of a set of double glass doors. The two sentries looked haggard and haunted with fatigue. Their faces were black with grime, their uniforms sweat-stained and putrid. One of the soldiers got on comms to report the relief-in-place, then turned and kicked aside one of the broken, hanging doors.

"Welcome to our nightmare, sir," the soldier said to Gillette. He was a corporal. His words sounded slightly slurred; evidence of the depths of his exhaustion. "We're glad you got across that damned river safely."

Above the door's lintel someone had scrawled the ominous message, *'Abandon all hope ye who enter here'*.

*

The relief-in-place proceeded smoothly under the direction of Mario Tonneguzzi. Charlie Company evacuated their posts and began wending their way wearily back across the ravaged ornamental gardens. When the XO reported to Gillette that Alpha Company had taken up their stations, he nodded curt acknowledgment then made an inspection of the building so he could survey the precarious position he had been asked to defend.

The apartment complex stood four stories high. On the rooftop, the XO had situated the company's M240 machine guns and one of the Javelin teams, supported by a handful of the unit's best riflemen. Gillette went to the waist-high wall that bordered the roof and peered thoughtfully out across the smoke scarred skyline.

The building stood on an intersection with a clear field of view westwards, over the riverside sector of the city, and to the north, towards the heart of the metropolis. Gillette's eyes slowly swept the horizon. A Chinese attack from the west would be dealt with by Bravo Company, who secured the adjoining complex. Any threat coming from the north was Alpha Company's responsibility. Gillette stared for a long time towards the heart of Dandong. Much of the city was a bomb-ravaged ruin of destroyed high-rise towers beneath a drifting pall of thick black smoke. Here and there fires burned, and the echo of distant artillery still reverberated – but for all the devastation and relentless far-away thunder of noise, there was a peculiar stillness about the scene that left Gillette with a vague sense of foreboding.

A wide arterial highway ran past the building, arrow-straight towards the heart of the city. The blacktop was littered with rubble and cratered in places but appeared to Gillette's eyes to still be serviceable. He frowned thoughtfully, then made an impulsive decision, based purely on instinct. He turned to Tonneguzzi.

"XO. See that building about three hundred yards to the north? The one with the spire on the roof and the reflective glass windows?"

Tonneguzzi came and stood beside Gillette. The XO peered, following the wide avenue with his eyes until he identified the site. It was an office block, about seven stories high. The buildings on either side had been flatted by artillery but the tall slim tower, though scarred and pitted with fragment damage, still stood.

"Yeah," the XO nodded.

"I want an OP set up on one of the top floors. Two men."

Tonneguzzi lifted an eyebrow in question. "Do we have orders for that? The Lieutenant Colonel was very specific about any provocation –"

Gillette cut the question off, his voice cracking like a whip. "I have orders to defend our position."

The abrupt petulant snap in Gillette's tone made the XO flinch. He nodded. "I'll see to it immediately, sir."

*

Every veteran knew that a combat soldier's life comprised endless hours of waiting followed by seconds of pure frantic fear.

The waiting was the worst part of the work.

But for the men of Alpha Company crouched in cover throughout the building standing post was a chance for small relief and respite after the violent terror of the bridge crossing. Some men not on duty took the opportunity to sleep. Others found quiet corners to read or pen letters to loved ones. The men standing post took advantage of the fraught silence to update the range cards for their weapons and performed basic weapons maintenance. Only Buck Gillette could not rest. He prowled the building, moving from story to story through the stairwells, personally checking each man's field of fire and their equipment.

"We're Alpha Company," he barked the mantra like an accusation when he found a young private crouched by a broken ground floor window, the soldier's field of fire obscured by the wreckage of a burned-out lorry on the street beyond the building. The young man had recently joined the unit and Gillette wasted no time making his expectations understood. "We do things once, and we do things well because we're the best damned unit in the division."

By late afternoon the company had settled into an uneasy routine. As dusk fell across the city and the sunset sky became lit with flares, the Chinese artillery suddenly opened fire, concentrating their thundering bombardment on the riverbank.

The allied engineers were using the twilight to move more bridge building equipment into position along the southern bank of the Yalu and the enemy were determined to make the work fraught with peril. The first enemy rounds arced across the sky, whistling in flight as they passed over the roof of the building where Gillette and Tonneguzzi stood watching. The artillery fire was coming from somewhere to the north, beyond the limits of the city, flashing and glowing orange against the horizon.

Gillette pressed a pair of binoculars to his eyes and peered north, but in the fading light could see little. He turned back towards the river and swept the powerful lenses in an arc, following the line of the riverbank. Explosions flashed and smoke roiled high into the darkening sky. The awesome fury of the Chinese barrage seemed to shake the air. As Gillette watched, a US Army supply truck was blown to pieces, and another lifted into the air and hurled end over end into the river.

Then the allied artillery began their counter-battery fire missions, and the night filled with a thundering madness as howling death criss-crossed the sky; a storm of fury that reminded Gillette of the battle for Seoul. He set the binoculars down and rubbed at his forehead like a man with a pounding headache.

"Any news from Battalion?"

The XO shrugged. "Nothing."

Gillette nodded, then sighed. He pressed the binoculars back to his eyes and swept the skyline north of the building one final time, still uneasy; still unable to shake off a sense of foreboding that continued to haunt him.

"Anything from the OP?"

"All quiet. Nothing to report," Tonneguzzi said.

Gillette made a frustrated face, then shrugged. He passed the binoculars to Tonneguzzi. Then suddenly the fatigue washed over him in a great wave so that he felt crushed by a weight of lethargy that made his legs heavy. He swayed on his feet. His mouth felt thick, and his words sounded slurred in his own ears.

"I'm going to sack out for a couple of hours. Wake me if anything – anything at all happens."

*

After just two hours of deathlike sleep, Gillette was suddenly and violently wrenched awake again by a crescendo of nearby savage explosions; dragged up through the layers of his exhaustion so that he groaned like a hungover drunk before he glanced at the luminous dial of his wristwatch.

The building was cloaked in darkness, and it took a moment for him to orientate himself. He stumbled to his feet and lurched towards the stairwell to search for Tonneguzzi.

Another explosion rocked the building and flung debris and shards of shrapnel at the walls. Somewhere ahead of him he could hear barked orders. He went towards the sound and finally found the XO, standing by a ruined west-facing window, peering out into the night.

"Are the Chinese attacking?" Gillette snapped, his fatigue from just moments ago thrust aside and replaced by an urgent surge of adrenalin.

"No," Tonneguzzi turned, surprised to see Gillette and silently shocked by his captain's haggard features. "It's ours. It's friendly fire. Some stupid bastard in the arty has fucked up his coordinates. Lieutenant Geyer is on comms trying to call the fire mission off."

"Christ!" Gillette shook his head. "Does Battalion know?"

"Yes. Reilly is trying to get through to Division to find out who called in the strike before we all get completely fubared."

Another artillery shell landed two hundred yards to the west, obliterating a small building and setting the ruins on fire. Gillette watched the leaping flames and the rising pall of smoke, silently fuming. Blue on blue casualties were an inevitable fact of war but it was a cruel way for a soldier to die. No warrior wanted to be killed by accidental friendly fire. Gillette bit down on a growl of frustration and was about to storm down the stairwell to find Lieutenant Geyer for a SITREP when the artillery bombardment stopped abruptly.

Gillette and Tonneguzzi stared at each other for long moments, holding their breath, waiting for explosions to resume. After a full minute Gillette allowed himself the luxury of relaxing.

"Go and get your head down for a few hours, XO. I'll oversee the men while you rest."

"But sir, you've not slept."

"Go," Gillette bristled. "That's an order."

In the absence of the XO, and the lack of any enemy activity, Gillette prowled the building like a haunting ghost, appearing unannounced amongst the troops standing post to inspect their equipment and admonish any man or woman who dared appear unalert.

"We're Alpha Company. We hold ourselves to a higher standard than the rest of the army," he berated one female corporal who had joined the company after the bloodbath of Seoul. "That's why we're the best damned unit in the division. If you can't keep up with the pace I'm setting and the level of excellence I demand, you should join the god-damned Air Force."

At midnight the sky suddenly burst into a fireworks spectacular of flares that hung high on the black horizon, illuminating the riverbank where the American engineers were frantically trying to construct new bridges. Gillette took the stairwell to the rooftop and watched the Chinese flares set the darkness aglow, anticipating a sudden violent aftermath of artillery fire – but it never came. After fifteen frantic minutes the sky turned dark again, and the eerie silence returned.

At 0400 hours Mario Tonneguzzi reappeared on the rooftop of the building, bleary-eyed but rested. He handed Gillette an aluminum canteen cup of hot coffee and the two men drank in companionable silence, staring northwards.

"The Chinese are up to something," Gillette brooded into the still night. "They're building for an attack."

Tonneguzzi wrapped his hands around his canteen cup and flicked his captain a speculative sideways glance. "There's been nothing on comms. No reports of enemy troop movement."

Gillette was not mollified. "Then our satellites aren't looking in the right places," he muttered, then tossed the dregs in the bottom of his mug over the side of the building.

He was about to hand over command to Tonneguzzi and retreat to the ground floor for more sleep when his RTO came bounding breathlessly up the stairs and burst onto the rooftop.

"The OP is reporting in," the radio operator thrust the handset at Gillette.

"Six-Six actual. Over."

"Six-Six, Two-Two," the men at the OP reported in, the caller's voice thick with urgency. "Enemy force in sight. Estimate two clicks to the north and approaching your position," Gillette heard the words crackle in his ear and felt a sudden sense of dreadful danger fizz in his blood.

"Two-Two, Six-Six. Estimate strength. Over!" he snapped.

From their elevated position several hundred yards north of the building, the two-man observer team had a clear view along the wide boulevard, the route backlit by burning ruins and the orange glow of flaring light from far away Chinese artillery. Their view in the darkness was enhanced by ENVG-B (Enhanced Night Vision Goggle-Binocular). The goggles used augmented reality to clearly identify targets in low-light situations and were issued to all front-line combat companies in the US Army.

After a tense pause the OP composed himself and delivered a more formal SALUTE report. The SALUTE format was a SITREP procedure typically followed by all OPs which included details about the *size* of the enemy force, the *activity*, the *location*, the enemy *unit* type, the *time* of the report being made and the *equipment* type; whether the enemy force included tanks, small arms, towed artillery or other equipment. The comprehensive format of a SALUTE ensured every relevant detail of the approaching threat was passed up the chain of command.

"Six-Six, Two-Two. Estimate enemy to be a mechanized infantry battalion in Type-08 APC's, supported by Type-96 MBT's. Over."

Gillette and Tonneguzzi exchanged an ominous glance. Gillette's grip on the radio handset was so tight his knuckles were white.

"Two-Two, Six-Six. How many tanks? Repeat how many tanks in support?"

There was a pause of crackling static that seemed to stretch on forever. Finally, the observer replied. "Six-Six, Two-Two. We see four Type-96s. Over."

"Roger, Two-Two. Evacuate your post ASAP. Out."

Gillette thrust the handset back to his RTO. His face was tight and set with tension, his eyes fixed with a simmering determination. "At least a battalion of mech infantry supported by a platoon of tanks," he summed up. "They're heading straight towards us."

"It could be some kind of feint," Tonneguzzi offered but Gillette shook his head, dismissing the suggestion.

"No. It's a Chinese attack. Maybe it's not a full-scale assault designed to push the army back into the river, but it's definitely an attack. My guess is the Chinese want to test our resolve. They want to press against our perimeter and see how we respond when they apply pressure."

He snatched for binoculars and pressed them to his eyes, peering into the darkness. He could just make out vague indistinct shapes far into the distance; a dense blackness moving inexorably closer, carried along on the rumble of heavy engines that burbled against the incessant dull reverberations of artillery fire.

For a tense, conflicted moment, Gillette hesitated – and then impulsively he made a snap decision.

"I'm going forward with a platoon of men, the two Javelin teams and one of the M240's," he said, a fever of determination in his eyes and his face working with tension. "We're going to ambush the bastards before they can organize themselves for an attack."

"What?" Tonneguzzi blanched, appalled. "We don't have orders –"

"And we don't have time to wait for orders, either," Gillette hissed. "By the time Lieutenant Colonel Reilly assesses the situation and makes a call, the Chinese will be swarming all over us. No," he shook his head with absolute conviction. "The only chance we have is to hit them before they hit us."

"Buck!" the XO resorted to Gillette's Christian name in a desperate attempt to appeal to his senses. "Man, you can't do this! We were ordered to remain strictly defensive. And a platoon isn't going to have enough firepower to take on an entire Chinese mech battalion. You'll get every man – including yourself – killed!"

"We're Alpha Company. We're not ordinary soldiers. We're the best warriors in the army," Gillette recited his mantra. "If anyone can do this, it's us. All we have to do is hit the Chinese hard and take out the tanks. If we pile the road up with twisted armor and dead bodies, the mech troops will withdraw."

"But we should notify HQ. Reilly needs to know what is happening in front of us."

Gillette shrugged. "Fine. Get HQ on comms and give Reilly a SITREP – but don't make the call until after I have exfiltrated the building."

"You'll get yourself and the entire platoon killed," Tonneguzzi made one last desperate appeal.

"If we do nothing, the entire company will be wiped out," Gillette shot back. He turned and dashed for the stairwell, barking for the Javelin team and two men serving the nearest M240 machine gun to follow him. The company's second Javelin team was attached to 3rd Platoon, defending the ground floor of the building. Gillette stood in the stairwell and growled in a loud booming voice.

"Third Platoon, on me! We're charging into harm's way. Move! Move! Move!"

*

With Gillette in the lead, running at full tilt, and 3rd Platoon following in his footsteps, the small knot of men filed from the building and ran towards the approaching Chinese armored column, using the rubble-strewn terrain of damaged office blocks that fringed the boulevard to conceal their approach. The Javelin crewmen and the MG team trailed the rest of the troops, doubled over by the weight of their weapons and the Javelin reloads they hefted.

From his vantage point on the rooftop, Mario Tonneguzzi watched the platoon move stealthily forward and felt a slither of apprehension twist in the pit of his guts. He shot a glance at the RTO and snapped his fingers. "Get Battalion HQ on the line. I need to send Lieutenant Colonel Reilly an urgent SITREP."

Down at ground level, Gillette's mind was racing and his heart thumped in his chest like a drum. He reached a section of highway that had been cratered by an errant allied artillery shell and paused intuitively. The deep crater had blown a hole in the side of the blacktop, reducing the width of the road to just five lanes. It would be a natural chokepoint where the enemy would be forced to slow and maneuver. It wasn't much, but it was his best chance. He turned and peered back towards the building where the rest of Alpha Company were dug in. He figured the distance at about four hundred meters. Then he looked north. The Chinese were advancing steadily, and through the lenses of his night vision goggles the approaching shapes were becoming more defined by the second. The vehicles in the vanguard were less than a mile away.

Gillette turned to the platoon and hissed his orders in a hoarse, strained voice. "This is it! Everyone spread out and find hard cover. Javelins to me!"

The men moved like wraiths in the darkness, looking for elevated positions from where they could pour down a fusillade of relentless fire on the enemy troops. The M240 team set up their machine gun behind a double brick wall that had once been the entrance to an underground parking garage. Gillette got his face close to the men who comprised the two Javelin teams.

"This is no fucking drill," he heard his voice in his own ears and the crackling savagery of his tone startled even him. "I want warheads on foreheads. Understand?"

The men nodded gravely but Gillette went on, hammering home his point.

"When I give the word, open fire and take out the four Chinese tanks first. Then hit the APCs. I want this entire roadway blocked with burning metal and bleeding bodies."

The crews dispersed and disappeared into the ruins. Gillette felt light-headed with a cocktail of emotions; his fear and tension bubbling to the surface. He was slick with the sweat of his exertions and his chest ached as if bound by tight steel bands. He dropped to his haunches and scrambled behind a mess of twisted steel and masonry just as the first enemy tank rumbled into clear view.

Directly overhead a single Chinese flare arced high into the pre-dawn gloom and then exploded, lighting the night.

It was the signal to unleash the dogs of war.

Chapter 3:

The two Javelin teams were spaced fifty paces apart, well protected atop mounds of building rubble. The operator closest to the approaching Chinese column set his weapon for a soft launch to camouflage his position. His partner was crouched nearby with a handful of reloads at his feet. The two-man team exchanged brief glances, sensing they were on the cusp of a pivotal moment that might ultimately be the death of them.

The operator flicked the ATTK/SEL switch on the handgrip of his CLU to change attack modes. The default setting on the FGM-148 was 'top attack' and had been designed for engaging enemy armored targets at distance of up to two-and-a-half thousand meters. The Chinese tanks and APCs were too close. The operator selected 'direct attack' and took a deep nerve-settling breath.

Then waited.

A flare arced across the sky then hung high in the air directly over the boulevard, bathing the advancing Chinese column in cold white light for several seconds. At the same instant, the four Type-96 tanks began to accelerate, their big engines whining and belching exhaust smoke.

"Open fire!" Gillette's voice could barely be heard over the great roar of mechanical noise and the jarring clatter of the tanks steel tracks.

The Javelin operator closest to the advancing enemy sucked in a last lungful of breath and held it. His index finger felt for the 'fire' trigger positioned on the right handgrip.

He squeezed.

The Javelin missile flew from the launch tube and flashed towards the enemy tanks, its solid fuel rocket throwing a bright streak of light across the sky. The Chinese tank commanders, buttoned down inside their steel turrets, had no time to react, or even recognize the danger. The projectile smashed into the lead Chinese tank, striking flush on the Type-96's front hull. The high-explosive anti-tank warhead detonated in a fiery thunderclap of flames, tearing through the steel hull and destroying the tank. The ruined vehicle ground to a sudden halt in the middle of the boulevard, slewed sideways and billowing great roiling clouds of black smoke. The savage *'boom!'* of the explosion shook the ground and filled the air with a haze of choking dust.

The second Javelin operator fired a heartbeat later, targeting the nearest remaining enemy tank just as the vehicle began to accelerate. The projectile flew from the launch tube like an unleashed arrow and smashed into the Type-96's undercarriage, demolishing the armored skirt, disintegrating steel track, the spinning drive sprocket, and several road wheels. The tank's engine bellowed like a beast struck a mortal blow, and then the vehicle became shrouded in smoke, backlit by bright flickering tongues of orange flame. Several seconds later a man emerged from the turret of the stricken tank, his clothes scorched and smoldering. He slithered, screaming through the smoke, his legs missing, his face pale and twisted in unimaginable agony until the tentacles of flame reached up over the hull and burned him to death.

The Type-96 was a second generation MBT that had entered service with the Chinese army during the late '90's. It was well armed, but its composite armor was no match for the killing power of the American Javelin.

In the stunned aftermath of the twin explosions, the Chinese column ground to a paralyzed halt. The two remaining MBT's split apart, veering wildly across the boulevard in opposite directions. One of the tanks accelerated and the other reversed, its turret turning towards where Gillette and 3rd Platoon were concealed.

Behind the tanks, the commanders and crewmen aboard the Type-08 APCs were struck dumb with shock, and then sheer terror. Anything that could so effortlessly destroy an MBT could certainly take out an APC with ease. The eight-wheeled vehicles had been introduced to the army twenty years earlier in a number of variants to handle infantry fire support missions, battlefield logistics and quick reaction operations. They were served by three-man crews and carried up to eleven infantrymen to the battlefront. The IFV variant was equipped with a 30mm autocannon and a 7.62mm coaxial machine gun. They had not been built for the fiery cauldron of frontline combat.

"Smoke! Smoke!" the Chinese commander leading the formation of Type-08s lunged for his radio and broadcast the urgent message across the battalion net. "Fire smoke!"

Some of the Type-08s simply stalled in the middle of the wide road. A few continued to roll forward, beginning to weave as they approached the destroyed tanks that lay strewn in their path. Most of the Chinese drivers tried to reverse away from the looming danger. Rear hatches were urgently swung open and Chinese infantry began to emerge down ramps onto the roadway.

"Fire!" Gillette screamed, and aimed his M4 carbine at a Chinese officer, waving his arms to urge the enemy infantry forward. The man was half-hidden from view, concealed by the hull of a Type-08. Gillette fired a short burst that clanged off the vehicle's steel armor and saw the Chinese officer flinch, then fling himself sideways out of sight.

"Fuck!" Gillette fired again, this time targeting two Chinese soldiers who were kneeling close together on the blacktop, gripped by confusion and disorientated. He hit one of the enemy soldiers in the head and the man was punched over and flung down onto the road. The second soldier fired blindly towards Gillette's position, then got to his feet and began to edge backwards in search of hard cover. Gillette shot the man in the chest. He was thrown against the hull of an APC, and then sagged slowly to the ground, his head hanging, his legs splayed, and his guts a bloody mess.

"Fire!" Gillette screamed again. He figured that six or maybe seven seconds had elapsed since the first Javelin had wreaked its savage toll. It would be at least another thirty seconds before the crews could reload their CLU launchers and fire again. This was the dangerous time; the perilous lulling moments when the Chinese could muster their infantry and make a concerted effort to overwhelm their ambushers. Momentum was critical in combat and Gillette knew that the fate of the attack hinged on his ability to keep the enemy confused and off balance.

The M240 roared to life, spitting death in a sweeping arc just as the first enemy troops mounted a counter-attack. A hundred mech infantrymen who had massed behind the shelter of their stalled APCs suddenly surged forward, led by a handful of brave officers. At the same moment the first Chinese 30mm autocannon roared into life, blazing a fusillade of wild fire in the direction of the ruins. The spray of autocannon fire flew well wide of Gillette and his men, but it was the first real act of Chinese defiance. The sudden flare of support fire bolstered the advancing infantry and put a roar into their throats as they swarmed across the blacktop.

The M240 scythed the Chinese down, killing indiscriminately. Some bullets whanged off the slab-sided hulls of the Type-08s, gouging livid scars into the steel. Other bullets tore into flesh, eviscerating the men, flensing limbs from bodies and spraying blood. A handful of Chinese soldiers in the vanguard of that first charge were bowled over in a great roar of bloody mayhem and left slithering and sobbing on the blacktop. The men behind them ran through the same pitiless hail of gunfire and fell in heaps on the ground. A Chinese officer, his leg drenched in blood and barely able to stand, valiantly barked at his troops to carry the fight to the enemy but was shot in the head.

"Hit the fuckers hard!" Gillette felt a surge of warrior savagery set light to his emotions. "Kill them all!"

The men of 3rd Platoon opened fire, their M4s blazing, lighting up the pre-dawn gloom in flickering spits of flaming death. One of the men tossed a grenade onto the wide street and it exploded beneath the wheels of a Type-08, disabling the vehicle. Grey clouds of haze began to drift across the battlefield as several of the reversing APCs popped off smoke canisters to conceal their attempt to retreat.

"Don't let them stand! Push them back!" Gillette felt the blood-lust overwhelm him.

One of the Javelins fired a second time. The warhead struck the reversing Type-96 tank while its turret was still turning. The percussive force of the close-proximity explosion clanged like the bells of hell and then a fiery heatwave washed across the battlefield. The Type-96 seemed to rock sideways beneath the hammer-blow force of the explosion, dislodging the huge turret from its seating and bending the long barrel. Fire brewed up from within the hull of the mangled tank and the screams of the burning men trapped inside the wreckage were shrill and chilling. Black smoke billowed into the sky and then a secondary explosion from somewhere within the vehicle blew the hull outwards and flung white-hot shrapnel flying in every direction.

"Jesus!" Gillette gasped in awe.

The ruined tank burned like a pyre, lighting the battlefield with weird flickers of light and leaping shadows. The M240 caught a squad of Chinese infantry just as they emerged from the rear door of their APC and mowed them down in three merciless seconds of thunderous fire.

The boulevard looked like a parking lot after a cyclone had weaved a dreadful path of destruction. Three of the Chinese tanks were ablaze and billowing smoke, and one of the APCs had been disabled. Several other troop carriers had been abandoned by their crews. The rest were slewed across the road, some firing their autocannons wildly into the darkness while others, their engines still running, sat idle and lumpen on the blacktop because there was nowhere to go. The road ahead was blocked by a carnage of twisted metal and the route back towards safety was jammed by trailing personnel carriers.

The last remaining Type-96 was struck broadside by a Javelin missile as the vehicle tried desperately to bulldoze its way forward through the mayhem. The warhead struck the hull, tore effortlessly through the armor plating, and exploded the engine compartment. The Chinese tank lurched to a sudden halt like a dog jerked violently back on its leash.

Gillette saw the enemy tank hit, saw the flash of searing light, and then felt the wall of heat wash over him along with a rising sense of elation and relief. He fired his M4 again at a Chinese soldier who lay wounded on the ground. The man had been struck by shrapnel and was writhing amidst the wreckage, scrabbling desperately at the blacktop with his clawed hands to drag himself into cover. Gillette shot the man twice and the body went suddenly limp.

At the rear of the stalled column, more enemy soldiers were massing behind the steel shelter of their APCs, pushed and cajoled into some semblance of order by senior officers. A half-dozen of type-08s began to roll slowly forward at low revs with their autocannons blazing.

Gillette saw the looming threat and realized intuitively that the tenor of the battle had changed. Up until that moment, the Americans had held the element of surprise. The shock and awe of the first frantic seconds of firing had given the platoon violent momentum, and the Chinese had been easy prey. Now the surprise had worn off and the enemy had begun to organize themselves to fight back.

Gillette barked at his Javelin teams and pointed towards the danger.

Dawn was breaking. The first pale light of the new day painted the belly of the clouds and washed over the fiery debacle, picking out the APCs and showing them as dark shapes against a watery grey backlight. One of the Javelin teams loosed a missile and it flew from the launch tube on a fluttering plume of exhaust. Two seconds later one of the advancing Type-08's was struck front-on, and the HEAT warhead blew the vehicle to pieces. The three-man crew were obliterated in the blink of an eye and the dozen Chinese infantrymen sheltering behind the APC were killed in the violent blast. The sound of the explosion echoed on the air like the impact of an artillery round.

The Americans hidden amidst the roadside rubble fired into the pall of smoke and flames, getting more hits. Belatedly, a Chinese autocannon atop another APC returned fire. An American private, firing his M4 from behind the cover of a damaged shopfront door, was struck full in the chest and killed instantly, knocked clean off his feet as if punched by an invisible fist. One of the men fighting nearby scrambled towards the body to render medical aid but doubled over and retched instead when he saw the steaming ruin of mangled flesh. A sergeant was hit in the head by shards of flying debris, slicing open his face so that a flap of flesh hung like a bloody joint of raw meat from his cheek. He fell backwards into the dirt with his jaw dislocated and a mouthful of broken teeth.

"Leave him!" Gillette snapped cruelly at two men who stopped firing to render aid.

Every one of Gillette's senses sang with savage triumph, a mad, malevolent light burning in his eyes. He sensed the Chinese were close to breaking. He tossed a grenade out onto the boulevard, and it exploded amongst the carnage, then he reloaded his M4 carbine with a few deft movements and fired again. The Chinese infantry at the rear of the convoy were still edging forward despite the loss of another Type-08. Gillette was just starting to wonder why the second Javelin team had not fired again when he heard a wicked retort and saw the blinding flash of light from the corner of his eye.

The Javelin missile streaked low across the blacktop and struck another Type-08 side on. The force of the explosion lifted the heavy troop carrier off its wheels and hurled it onto its side, wrenching the hull apart. More enemy soldiers died. More were wounded. One Chinese infantryman appeared through the choking clouds of smoke, staggering, his uniform on fire, his arms flailing. The man screamed in great explosive gusts of agony. The obscene stench of burning flesh choked in Gillette's throat. The burning man dropped to his knees and the sounds of his wretched death became rattling groans until one of the American soldiers shot the man, putting an end to his grotesque torture.

"Keep shooting!" Gillette urged his men on to greater effort and lobbed more grenades into the cauldron of fiery chaos. Another American rifleman was wounded, struck by a hail of Chinese machine gun fire. The man threw down his M4 and clutched at his shoulder, blood oozing through his fingers and his face wrenched in pain. Gillette, caught up in the madness of the moment, turned and snarled savagely at the stricken man, ruthless spite in his eyes.

"Get back in the fight!" he spat at the bleeding soldier. "Keep firing!"

*

Standing on the rooftop of the building several hundred yards to the south with binoculars pressed to his eyes, Mario Tonneguzzi peered into the pre-dawn gloom and listened tensely as the firefight unfolded.

The Chinese tanks exploding under the wicked lash of Javelin missiles lit the night sky in a series of searing fireballs and the thunder-like rumble of the ear-shattering blasts seemed to echo on the air. Tonneguzzi could identify the sounds of American M4s firing and the ripping-like roar of the Chinese autocannons as they fired back. He heard grenades explode and watched the dawn fill with towers of black oily smoke.

Every remaining man in Alpha Company was on high alert and the company's mortars had been set up in the churned earth of the ornamental park under Lieutenant Geyer's command, awaiting the call for support fire.

Lieutenant Colonel Reilly appeared on the rooftop, grim-faced and silently seething. Charlie Company, who had been resting away from the front line, had been ordered to reinforce the building in case the Chinese broke through the ambush.

Reilly and Tonneguzzi exchanged bleak glances.

"Well?" the Lieutenant Colonel's face was hard as granite, and there was a bitter tone of menace in his voice as he regarded the company XO.

"3rd Platoon are putting up one hell of a fight," Tonneguzzi gave his opinion.

"Casualties?"

"Some," the XO admitted, "although exact details are still unconfirmed. Two wounded, at least." The platoon RTO had opened a comms link back to the company HQ and had kept it hot throughout the firefight, reporting the destruction of the four enemy tanks as well as fragmented casualty reports.

Reilly went to the low wall that bordered the rooftop and peered into the smoke-filled distance. The shallow cough of small arms fire and the juddering rattle of machine guns echoed off the walls of rubble and sounded strangely hollow to his ears. Day was beginning to dawn across the city and the far horizon showed a flash of glowing orange light. A moment later the sound of enemy artillery shells whistling through the air on their lethal trajectory carried clearly. Involuntarily, Reilly turned and peered south, towards the river. During the night the allies had constructed several more float bridges and already troops and equipment were gathering in the vehicle parks, awaiting orders to make the perilous crossing over the Yalu.

Reilly winced, muttered a fervent prayer, and then turned back to the battle taking place right in front of him as the Chinese shells began to fall, pounding the riverbank and trembling the air.

He had the entire battalion on alert and a comms line open to an artillery battery who were waiting at their howitzers several miles behind the front lines, on standby for possible fire missions. He withered Tonneguzzi with another malevolent glare.

"Captain Gillette clearly understood my orders, correct?"

"Yes, sir," the XO nodded.

"He understood that Alpha Company's mission was to defend this building and remain strictly defensive."

"Yes, sir."

*

"Dodds! Harrigan! Go forward! Get into that rubble by the roadside and pin those bastards down!" Gillette roared at the M240 crew, pointing threateningly down the road to where perhaps a hundred or more Chinese infantry were gathering for an assault. Gillette could feel the momentum of the firefight slowly turning against him. The Chinese had an overwhelming numerical infantry advantage and now they had recovered from the shock of the ambush, the vehicle crewmen who served the turret-mounted 30mm autocannons aboard the surviving Type-08s were beginning to force the Americans deeper into cover with torrents of well-aimed fire.

Another Type-08, standing stationary in the middle of the boulevard, was blown apart by a Javelin missile, the fireball from the explosion so intense that it scorched the blacktop and melted tar. Flaming rivulets of fuel trickled into the gutters to mingle with blood and gore. A Chinese soldier crouched on the far side of the road was decapitated by flying shrapnel and another was hit by smoldering debris.

A noise like a blaring trumpet suddenly sounded over the chaotic clamor of the battlefield, and then – instead of rushing forward to overwhelm the Americans – the massing Chinese infantry, incredibly, began to fall back.

For a long, bewildered moment Gillette doubted his eyes.

"The Chinese are retreating!" a single voice broke through the stunned, silent aftermath.

"Yes," Gillette said. "We've won. We've beaten the bastards," his voice was choked with violent satisfaction. Triumph and overwhelming relief sang savagely within him, swelling and bursting in his chest so that he could hardly draw breath. He watched the enemy infantry withdraw and then the surviving Type-08s joined the rout.

Around Gillette the men of 3rd Platoon slowly emerged from the rubble, like the survivors of some dreadful natural disaster. They were cut and bleeding, limping and haggard with fatigue, their faces thick with grime and sweat, and their eyes red-rimmed. Some sobbed with relief, others simply sat and shook with the trembling after-effects of their terror.

Gillette felt himself become overwhelmed by a gloating sense of vindication, certain that his bold pre-emptive ambush had averted disaster for the entire battalion. He felt ten feet tall and bulletproof.

The platoon withdrew towards the building where the rest of the company waited, Gillette swaggering at the head of the column and the rest of the men trailing him. At the rear of the small bedraggled line of warriors came the dead and the wounded, carried on litters.

Men defending the ground floor of the building rushed out into the pale dawn light to help tend to the injured. Tonneguzzi stood amongst them. Gillette peeled off his helmet and wiped his brow on the sleeve of his uniform.

"Send up a 9-line," he told the XO somberly. "Sergeant Wallace was struck in the face and Culver was shot in the chest. The boy might not make it."

A 9-line was the format of a radio request for wounded personnel to be medevacked out of a combat zone. Tonneguzzi nodded obediently and dashed away in search of the RTO. Gillette swallowed a mouthful of water and then felt himself begin to deflate, gripped by a sudden sense of exhaustion. He had barely rested in the past two days and now his strung-out nerves were frayed and brittle. He sagged down to the ground amongst the survivors of 3rd Platoon and – despite the urgent triage work going on all around him – lapsed into a fitful sleep.

*

Gillette woke three hours later – jerked alert by a rising crescendo of explosions and gunfire. He sat up instinctively and reached for his weapon, even before his mind had time to cut through the cottonwool of his fatigue.

The ground floor of the building appeared deserted, though he could see blood spatters in the dirt and the leftover rubbish of field dressing kits. He came unsteadily to his feet, moving with the arthritic stiffness of an old man, and peered out through the nearest doorway. All he could see was a sky filled with black smoke.

He hobbled towards the stairwell, the stiffness of tired limbs making him wince. When he reached the rooftop of the building Tonneguzzi was there, binoculars pressed to his eyes.

Without taking the high-powered lenses from his face, the XO said, "Feel better?"

"I feel like shit," Gillette growled. "What the fuck is happening?"

"Our tanks have broken through the Chinese frontlines," Tonneguzzi explained. "Two hours ago, they mounted an attack in Yianbao District and punched a hole through the enemy's perimeter."

Gillette snatched possessively for the binoculars and peered east. The elevated view from the rooftop gave him a glimpse of the Yalu and a strip of riverbank buildings beneath a wide front of black oily smoke. Moving like insects in the distance he could see Abrams tanks advancing, guns and smoke cannisters firing. The sounds of explosions rose and fell on the fluky breeze, a noise like berserk drummers beating an apocalyptic frenzy.

"The Chinese are retreating?" Gillette set down the binoculars and sounded astonished.

"They're falling back," Tonneguzzi moderated. "This morning Command pushed an entire brigade of troops across several float bridges further along the river, supported by a column of mechanized infantry. They linked up with the Abrams tanks we already had on the northern bank and launched a surprise attack through the main streets of Yianbao."

Gillette felt a lift of relief. If the momentum of the breakout could be maintained, and if the allies could continue to quickly funnel fresh troops across the river and into the combat zone, the Chinese would be forced to retreat deeper into the city.

Between the massive earth-shaking explosions of artillery and the violent crack of Abrams tank fire, the sound of small-arms coughed and spluttered sporadically. Gillette guessed the closest fighting was happening perhaps two miles eastward of his position, but still he turned to Tonneguzzi expectantly.

"What are our orders?" he asked quickly, the fatigue sloughing away to be replaced by a warrior's rising sense of anticipation.

"Orders?" the XO frowned.

"Is the battalion going to be part of the advance?"

Tonneguzzi shook his head and shrugged. "We've had no word from brigade - but Lieutenant Colonel Reilly wants us both at HQ in an hour's time. I guess we'll find out then."

*

Gillette was struck by an ominous sense of funereal foreboding as he and Mario Tonneguzzi were ushered into Lieutenant Colonel Reilly's makeshift office.

Reilly looked up from behind his desk, and his face tightened with a veiled expression of distaste. He regarded both men coldly for long silent seconds before he finally spoke.

"Four men dead and six seriously wounded," he flicked his eyes down to a sheaf of papers on his desk, then fixed his gaze on Gillette. "That's the price Alpha Company paid for that little stunt you pulled this morning."

Gillette felt himself bristle but said nothing. Lieutenant Colonel Reilly rose slowly from his desk and threw down his pen. "An entire squad of soldiers either killed or so badly wounded they're out of action."

Gillette felt his temper rise, but he had the good sense to hold it in check. This meeting wasn't happening the way he had expected. Reilly, instead of being pleased with the success of the dawn ambush, seemed on the verge of exploding.

The Lieutenant Colonel was standing over his desk, his fists clenched.

"Were my orders to you not clear, Captain Gillette?" He snatched up the sheet of paper containing the casualty list and held it out.

Gillette opened his mouth and then closed it again.

"Well?" Reilly demanded.

"Sir, I believe I acted in the best interests of the battalion," Gillette said stiffly.

"In the best interests of the battalion, or your ego? You couldn't help yourself, could you? You had to play the hero, and in the process, you destroyed almost a full fighting platoon of men."

"The casualties are regrettable," Gillette was stung by the exaggeration.

"Regrettable?" Reilly's eyes seemed to bulge, and his mouth wrenched into an ugly slash. "Those deaths and injuries were *avoidable!*"

"Sir, I disagree," Gillette stiffened, and his own expression soured as he defended his actions. "I judged the looming threat of the advancing Chinese armored column so serious that it justified the need for immediate action."

"And who put you in command of the battalion? Who made you the decision-maker in this unit? Who gave you the authority to act on your own god-damned initiative after my explicit orders were for you to remain defensive?"

"Sir, I know –"

"You know?" Reilly came from behind his desk and prowled across the room, seething, his face working in anger. "You think you know everything about soldiering, captain. That's why you're a bad officer. You have an inflated opinion of your own leadership skills and your ability to command men."

"Sir, I got the result," Gillette snapped. "The Chinese column was routed before it could launch an attack against my company's position. If left unchecked, the enemy tanks could have punched through our lines and ravaged the entire battalion."

"So, you took it upon yourself to play the god-damned hero."

"It wasn't a matter of heroics," Gillette spat back, the two men squaring off and the tension in the room so thick that Mario Tonneguzzi feared physical violence was imminent. "It was a question of leadership. The Chinese were a direct and immediate threat of overwhelming force. Using my judgment, I deemed an ambush was the best way to re-take the initiative and to thwart an impending attack."

"You don't have a high enough pay grade to make those decisions, captain. Your first reaction should have been to alert me."

"Sir, there was no time," Gillette said stubbornly.

"Tell that to the wives and families of the men who died carrying out your impulsive plan," Lieutenant Colonel Reilly hissed. "I'm sure it will be a great comfort to the widowed and the grieving."

Gillette swayed as though he had been slapped across the face. His hands were held low by his side, his fists bunched. His eyes were alight with a bitter seething resentment and his lips drew back tight, baring his teeth.

"Sir, I personally alerted HQ," Tonneguzzi interjected, trying to diffuse the tension.

"Yes. But only *after* Captain Gillette had already exfiltrated the building and gone forward to mount his ambush!" Reilly roared.

The sound of the CO's voice cracked around the walls of the room like the echo of a gunshot. Reilly took a step back, exerting all his willpower to restrain himself. He paced the room for several minutes, breathing raggedly until he could regain some level of composure while Gillette and Tonneguzzi stood rigid and white faced in the eye of the storm.

Finally, Reilly turned on his heel. He seemed suddenly tired; as though the last ounces of energy had been wrung from him. His shoulders slumped and he sighed like a weary man at the end of a long journey.

"Third Battalion has been ordered to withdraw back across the Yalu at dawn tomorrow morning," Reilly spoke softly. "We're being moved twenty clicks northeast for another mission. British and Canadian troops will be moving into our sector later tonight to relieve us."

Gillette could not help himself. He looked appalled. "Excuse me, sir," he blurted. "Do you mean to say that our boys took all the risks, suffered all the casualties and endured all the hardships of holding the bridgehead – and now the lousy Canadians and Brits are going to come swanning in to take all the credit for our sacrifice?"

Reilly glared back, scandalized with dismay. "We are a team, Captain Gillette," the CO said with forced patience through tightly gritted teeth. "Maybe you don't understand that. There is no room in this man's army for wannabe heroes or reckless glory-hunters who crave medals and recognition. Sometimes you're ordered to play tight end. Sometimes you have to play wide receiver. And once in a while you get to quarterback the game. We have our orders. We're being benched. Now get out of my sight and inform your men. Dismissed."

Chapter 4:

Gillette summoned his company's leadership team to the ground floor of the building thirty minutes later to issue his Warning Order.

The platoon leaders and sergeants were haggard and unkempt from the ceaseless hours of tension they had endured. Lieutenant Geyer stood with his FIST sergeant at the edge of the gathering, both men listening intently. The Fire Support Team sergeant was a huge hulking black man from Alabama with a penchant for chewing tobacco and colorful language. Mario Tonneguzzi stood behind Gillette's shoulder with a serious expression on his face. It was to him that the burden of logistics for the company's transport would fall.

Gillette acknowledged each man with a curt nod, and then brusquely outlined the situation. He was seething with indignation, Lieutenant Colonel Reilly's scathing criticism of his pre-dawn ambush still ringing loudly in his ears. His fuming resentment put an edge of bitterness in his voice as he issued his instructions.

"Alpha Company has been ordered to evacuate our position at midnight tonight," he announced, and saw dawning dismay creep across the faces of the assembled men. They stirred restlessly and shuffled their feet in the dirt. "The entire battalion has been ordered back across the Yalu. Brigade has another combat mission for us twenty clicks to the northeast of Dandong. A convoy of vehicles will meet us on the North Korean side of the river to provide transport to our next area of operations."

"We only just dug in, sir," the FIST sergeant complained, his voice rumbling like thunder.

"What about our casualties, sir? We've had no word of replacements yet," the lieutenant leading 3rd Platoon protested. The medevac of Sergeant Wallace following the gruesome facial injuries he had received during the ambush had left the platoon short of a steady leader and several riflemen.

Tonneguzzi cut across the discussion to placate the officer. "Battalion has requested replacement troops to bring us back up to strength. They will meet us at the rendezvous point over the Yalu River."

The 3rd Platoon lieutenant grunted while the other leaders exchanged perplexed glances. The 1st Platoon lieutenant shook his head.

Gillette shrugged, disgruntled, then added the last damning piece of news. "We're being relieved by Canadians and British troops."

"Fucking Canadians and Brits? When did this god-damned war turn into a tea party?" Lieutenant Geyer blurted the complaint.

The FIST sergeant spat a wad of tobacco juice into the dirt and wiped his mouth with the sleeve of his uniform. He muttered a string of scornful expletives under his breath and shook his head.

Gillette shared his men's loathing contempt for the allied troops fighting alongside the US forces but compelled himself to restraint. Instead, he cunningly appealed to the men's pride as an expedient way to divert their umbrage at the news.

"When the going gets tough..." Gillette began.

"The army calls on Alpha Company!" the men chorused as one, repeating one of their captain's oft-spoken mantras.

"That's right," Gillette warmed to his version of events. "It seems like all the hard work in Xhenxing District has been done, so the B-team is coming in to mop up, while we get shipped out to where the next real fight is going to happen."

Gillette's perversion of the facts seemed to mollify the company's leaders. A few moments ago, they had been sullen and downcast. Now there was a re-igniting of resolve and determination in their eyes.

"We're the best god-damned company the US Army has to offer," Gillette reminded them, making eye contact with each man as he looked about the small group. "If it was easy, the army wouldn't need us. Hooah!"

"Hooah!"

*

The relief-in-place happened in the dead of night. A column of Canadian infantry took over Alpha Company's positions, watched with simmering contempt by the veteran American soldiers who huddled amongst themselves and sniggered with adversarial scorn whenever the newly-arrived officers issued orders. The Canadian troops were clean-shaven and wearing clean uniforms. They looked, to the hard-faced men of Alpha Company, like they had just stepped off a parade ground.

"Toy soldiers," one of the American riflemen said in a deliberate stage whisper, certain he would be overheard.

"Probably never even seen a Chinese or North Korean since they joined the fighting," another rifleman joined in the spiteful banter.

"Jesus! Did these Canucks sail to war on a cruise ship?" one of the men from a Javelin team studied the allied troops with thinly veiled incredulity.

Gillette stood in a corner on the ground floor with his arms folded and watched the Canadians take up their posts in surly silence until Mario Tonneguzzi reported to him.

"The Canadian captain wants a quick word with you before we exfil to the bridges," the XO said discreetly.

"Tell him I'm busy," Gillette sulked.

Tonneguzzi made a face that might have been a look of disapproval, or perhaps appeal. "Buck…"

Gillette sighed theatrically and snarled. "Fine."

When Tonneguzzi returned he had a young fresh-faced captain with sandy blonde hair and a boyish grin of eagerness in tow. Gillette withered the Canadian officer with a glare, noting his tidy well-rested appearance.

"You wanted to see me?" he growled.

"Hi, yes," the Canadian thrust out his hand amiably. "Captain Devon French, 3rd Battalion, PPCLI – Princess Patricia's Canadian Light Infantry."

"Princess *what?*" Gillette looked aghast. He had never heard of such a title for a fighting unit. The regimental name seemed to perfectly encapsulate his loathing opinion of America's fighting allies.

"Princess Patricia's Canadian Light Infantry. Most people refer to us as the 'Patricias' or the 'Pats'. We take our name from Princess Patricia of Connaught, daughter of the Governor General of Canada back in 1914," the young man explained.

Gillette eyed the man coldly. "What do you want?"

"A SITREP," the smile of friendliness slowly slid off the face of the Canadian soldier.

Gillette grunted. "You want a situation report? Okay, fine. All the real fighting has been done before you arrived – by Alpha Company," he said through gritted teeth. "There are four burned out Chinese T-96s and just as many enemy APCs on the road directly north of the building, about six hundred meters away. There are about fifty dead Chinese soldiers lying scattered on the road amongst the wreckage. We caused all that death and destruction this morning with a single platoon of men. That's all you need to know."

*

The march back to the riverbank was uneventful, but fraught with horrific reminders of how fierce the fighting had been to establish the allied bridgehead. The men trudged wearily past the burned-out hulks of two Abrams tanks and more than a dozen Chinese T-96s. Dead bodies littered the ground, some in small heaps where the house-to-house fighting had been at its fiercest. The corpses were bloated and bullet-riddled. Rats scurried and scampered amidst the remains.

The streets were deserted, except for the occasional allied patrol. Most of the buildings had been reduced to rubble but here and there some low-rise structures still stood, their windows blackened, and glass shattered. The air stank of oily smoke and raw sewerage. Flares arced across the sky, lighting the way.

The closer they marched towards the river, the louder the sounds of men and heavy machinery became until they stepped out of the city's shadows and into clear view of the river.

Gillette paused for a moment and gaped.

As a child he had seen grainy black-and-white photos of the D-Day landings at Normandy during World War 2; images of men spilling from landing craft, fighting on the beaches, and pictures of soldiers pushing inland against a backdrop of LCVPs and small warships. It was the only reference for what he saw now; columns of Abrams tanks and Humvees pouring across the river on a dozen flat bridges while, on the northern bank of the Yalu, infantry units were forming up and preparing to push deeper into the city – all beneath a veil of drifting smoke and the roar of fighter jets overhead. It was a massive operation involving thousands of men and machines – evidence that the Chinese had given up the fight to hold the allies advance and that a new deadly phase of the battle for Dandong would soon begin.

The Divisional MPs around the bridgehead were charged with maintaining order amidst all the clamor, chaos and confusion of a night crossing. A corporal approached Alpha Company bearing the harried, frazzled expression of a shop clerk at the height of Christmas Day sales.

Gillette spoke briefly and heatedly to the MP, and then Tonneguzzi joined the conversation, playing peacekeeper.

"Bridge Five," the MP relented and pointed east. "But stay in single file and keep to the right guide rail – unless you want to get caught in the crush."

Other infantry units were also part of the trickling exodus back into North Korea. The soldiers that had held the frontline looked exhausted and lumpen, filthy with grime, trudging southwards like dead men on leaden feet. Freshly arriving troops crammed aboard transport lorries peered out from their vehicles with a mixture of awe and foreboding as they headed into the combat zone.

Once the company reached the south side of the river more waiting MPs directed the weary column of men to rest areas beyond the battlefront where aid stations were set up and Brigade Support Battalion (BSB) troops dispensed hot meals and coffee from a scatter of mess tents.

The company of weary troops dropped exhausted into the long grass. They were hungry, dizzy with sleep-deprivation, and made haggard by the depths of their exhaustion. Their uniforms were thick with mud and spattered with blood. The ripe stench of their bodies was the accumulation of days of sweat and unending tension.

Crews from the mess tent wandered around the makeshift encampment dispensing MREs and tin trays of hot food, and a chaplain clutching a bible to his chest drifted between the men, offering kind words of comfort and the opportunity to pray. Gillette found a soft patch of long grass and threw himself down with a death-like sigh, only now becoming aware of the depths of his fatigue. His hands shook slightly, and his legs trembled. His eyes felt gritty, and filth clung to him in caked layers. He had not shaved or bathed in days, sleeping only fitfully, eating little. He yawned and every muscle in his body seemed to groan in protest.

Mario Tonneguzzi loomed out of the darkness with a tray of hot food and a Styrofoam cup of coffee. The XO handed the food and drink to Gillette and glanced at the luminous dial of his watch.

"0300," he muttered. "The convoy will be here in three hours."

Gillette grunted around a mouthful of food, wolfing down hot stew with the famished abandon of a starving man. He closed his eyes, savoring the first proper meal he had eaten in days, then washed it down with a mouthful of coffee.

Tonneguzzi sat in the grass by his side and picked at the food on his own tray. The chaplain paused in front of them, but Gillette waved the man away. He had seen too much evil and violence to believe in a god. The chaplain smiled benevolently and drifted off into the darkness.

"Convoy vehicles?" Gillette spoke around a mouthful of food.

Tonneguzzi shrugged. "I asked for limousines and a private jet, but I doubt we'll get them," he mocked and then turned serious. "Probably Oshkosh MAT-Vs and M1083 trucks."

MAT-V was the way the troops typically pronounced M-AVT because it rolled off the tongue more readily and sounded more like 'Humvee' – the vehicle the Oshkosh was in the process of replacing through the US Army.

Gillette swallowed the food in his mouth and ran his hand across his jowls, feeling the rasping stubble of his beard. The notion of shaving flittered across his mind, but he dismissed the idea. He was simply too tired to care.

"What about the rest of the battalion? When do they pull out and follow us to the rendezvous point?"

"Later tonight," the XO said. "They will be relieved by some Brits and then trucks will carry them northeast to meet up with us."

"We have to prepare the ground and set up a perimeter?" Gillette frowned. "We're frontline soldiers, not fucking engineers."

"No. Reilly said the site is set up, about a mile south of the river, surrounded by forest. Support staff are already there prepping the location."

"Okay," the news placated Gillette enough for him to set aside his ire and continue eating. He drained his cup of coffee and stretched out in the grass. "Wake me at 0545 hours."

*

The fleet of M-ATVs and heavy trucks arrived at the rest point just after 0600 hours. Alpha Company were waiting, standing in lines, burdened with their kit and equipment, when the lead vehicles appeared through the trees. It was dawn on the Korean peninsula, the first light of a new day that seemed to promise hot and oppressive conditions.

The men clambered aboard their transports and after a short delay the vehicles pulled away in belches of exhaust smoke, headed north east. From the Oshkosh that was Gillette's command vehicle, he peered ahead into the forested distance. The M-ATV was trundling along at low revs behind the four vehicles transporting 1st Platoon at the head of the convoy, with the rest of the company, the FIST team, the mortar team and the medics near the tail of the procession.

Gillette felt fidgety and frustrated, still bitterly aggrieved that his men had been pulled out of Zhenxing District at the precise moment when the army were preparing to push deeper into the city. The allies would need elite fighting men like Alpha Company if the Chinese were to be pushed out of the city, he felt certain, and Gillette resented the lost opportunity to show off his leadership skills. Instead, they were being sent twenty miles to the north east into a wilderness of forest on some half-assed mission that history would never remember. He sulked down low in his seat and peered sullenly out through the windows.

The route was a scruffy forest trail that clung to the sides of the hills and serpentined through narrow shadow-shrouded valleys. The trees pressed in from every side, blotting out the light. They passed through a drab little village that had been carved out of the surrounding forest. The settlement comprised just a dozen meager huts with thatched roofs. The bedraggled peasants who eked out a living from small vegetable gardens came out to line the road, their expressionless faces veiling hostility. A mangy dog barked savagely at the American trucks as they passed and was run over by one of the Oshkosh M-ATV's and left dead by the roadside.

Nothing of what he saw seemed to register with Gillette. He stared fixedly ahead, brooding over the unfairness of army life – until the landscape around him altered and suddenly the vehicles were changing down through the gears to tackle a steep mountain rise.

The speed of the convoy slowed to a dangerous crawl and at last Gillette's instincts screamed a dutiful warning. He sat upright and studied the thick forest on either side of the road.

"Six-Six to all vehicles," he snatched for the radio mic mounted to the IAN/PRC-117G multiband radio on the vehicle's dashboard. "Weapons ready for a possible ambush. Acknowledge."

The radio crackled through a series of confirmations. Gillette reached for his M4 and rested the weapon on his lap. It was possible that troops from the shattered North Korean army had retreated in the aftermath of the fighting and were now in this wilderness border region, or perhaps even trying to cross the Yalu into China to continue the fight against the allies.

The tension in the slow-moving procession became palpable. The sound of the vehicles grinding up the winding dirt track seemed to echo loudly throughout the forest, drowning out the birds. An eerie sense of foreboding pressed close around the column.

The convoy broke from the shadows and burst into bright sunlight two hundred meters from the summit of the steep hill and Gillette had a brief but breathtaking view of the terrain for miles in every direction. Through the fringe of trees, he could see the Yalu River, glittering like a band of beaten silver in the sunlight, and he could see the undulating canopy of tree-tops, like humping green waves that stretched away towards the east for miles. It was a breathtaking vista of natural beauty, spoiled only by the dark scars of black cloud that hung low on the horizon; evidence that the fight for Dandong went on without him.

Gillette flicked a glance at his vehicle's driver and noted that the Oshkosh had been slowed to a crawl. An enemy machine gun, hidden within the cover of the forest, could tear the convoy to pieces in just a few short savage seconds.

He leaned out through the window of the Oshkosh and peered past the four vehicles in the vanguard of the column. He figured the convoy was still a hundred paces from the summit of the rise. It was the perfect place for a surprise enemy attack. He felt his breath catch in his throat and a surge of adrenalin set his senses alight.

He snatched for the radio mic again.

"Two-Six, Six-Six," he got on comms to the 2nd Platoon leader whose four troop-transport vehicles were at the tail of the convoy.

"Six-Six, Two-Six," the platoon lieutenant answered quickly.

"Two-Six, dismount your men. I want them on foot on both sides of the column and on high alert until we crest this rise. Over."

"Six-Six, Roger," the lieutenant acknowledged.

It was perhaps excessive caution, but Gillette felt better for having issued the order. A veil of armed infantry walking beside the vehicles might dissuade an enemy attack. His prudent action might not be worthy of mention in a report, but if the North Koreans sprang an ambush and he had not taken precautions, he knew he would be crucified for reckless dereliction of his duties, and Gillette had no intention of blemishing his combat record through oversight.

The riflemen from 2nd Platoon dismounted from their trucks and came forward, walking alongside the lead vehicles in the convoy like they were on patrol, until the first Oshkosh finally reached the summit and began the subsequent descent. Gillette let out an exhalation of relief and relaxed a little. 2nd Platoon re-mounted their vehicles and the road ahead of the convoy plunged back down into tree-covered shadow. Gillette set his M4 down and flicked a glance at his driver.

"How much longer?"

The young driver hesitated, the shrugged his shoulders. "An hour, sir," he guessed. "If we don't strike trouble."

*

Trouble struck just a few minutes later.

The ambush was so perfectly executed that, even in the midst of the terror, the turmoil and the violent explosions, Gillette felt a stabbing prickle of grudging appreciation for the enemy's merciless cunning.

The attack came at the bottom of the steep descent, when the convoy of vehicles were in low gear, their big tires scrabbling for grip on the loose gravel surface. Just as the lead Oshkosh was engulfed in deep forest shadow, two men burst from the fringe of dense undergrowth. They were North Korean soldiers, their uniforms filthy tattered rags, their eyes crazed with berserker fanaticism. Each man had a canvas satchel slung over their shoulders. The first North Korean threw himself in front of the lead M-ATV, screaming with maniacal incoherence.

The driver behind the wheel of the Oshkosh instinctively stomped his foot on the brake but the lieutenant commanding 1st Platoon, sitting in the passenger seat, roared a warning.

"Floor it!" he screamed, "Go! Go! Go!"

Time seemed to stop.

The driver saw the enemy soldier reach one hand into the satchel, saw the savage malevolence in the man's eyes, recognized, too, the man's suicidal intent. He crushed the gas pedal flat to the floor and the Oshkosh leaped forward like a wild horse, skidding out of control. The first ambusher was struck front-on and flung into the air, thrown tumbling over the hood of the M-ATV, arms and legs flailing, his body cartwheeling end over end by the crushing impact. He landed on the shoulder of the road, crumpled and bleeding.

The second North Korean timed his attack on the third Oshkosh in the line, springing from the shadows at the verge of the road and launching himself towards the vehicle as it inevitably slowed. He had the strap of the satchel in his hand, and he slung it side armed, sending the bag skidding across the dirt, beneath the wheels of the M-ATV. The driver braked hard and wrenched the vehicle's wheel. The Oshkosh slewed off the road and collided into a tree.

The gunner on the vehicle's mounted M240 machine gun swiveled the weapon and hosed the surrounding wall of forest, firing blindly into the gloom, jacked up on adrenalin and raw terror.

The entire column braked urgently to a halt and those men who were alert to the danger in the vanguard of the convoy braced themselves for the inevitable explosions.

The canvas satchel on the roadway had ripped open, revealing a handful of heavy rocks. The realization that the attack had been some kind of insane ruse began to dawn on the Americans and relief washed over them. Through the sudden blurt of panicked radio chatter, Gillette heard a crackle and then the voice of 1st Platoon's lieutenant. "Bogus IED."

At which point the North Koreans launched their real attack.

There were four North Korean soldiers armed with assault rifles, hidden in the trees on the opposite side of the dirt trail. They opened fire on the convoy from close range, peppering the vehicles at the front of the column. An M-ATV gunner manning his M240 went down, shot in the back of the head and killed instantly. The driver of a truck was struck in the neck. Blood spattered the windshield of the vehicle as the driver was thrown sideways inside the cabin. The sergeant in the passenger seat ducked down into cover a split-second before a fury of bullets drummed like a hailstorm against his door.

"We're under attack!" the sergeant snatched for the vehicle's radio and broadcast across the company net.

Gillette felt his blood turn chill. He snatched for his M4 and barked orders to his vehicle's gunner. "Spray the forest. Open fire!"

A North Korean lobbed a grenade onto the road. It exploded under the chassis of the lead Oshkosh, but the vehicle's mine-resistant bodywork protected the crewmen inside. Dust boiled from beneath the vehicle as the impact of the explosion lifted the front end of the M-ATV briefly into the air.

The panicked driver gunned the engine and drove through a final flurry of enemy bullets, fighting to keep the vehicle on the road until he had run the gauntlet and was out of range. He skidded the Oshkosh to a halt and the gunner swiveled his weapon around and opened fire.

Men began spilling out of the trucks at the rear of the convoy, coming down the gravel slope, slipping and skidding to keep their balance. The North Koreans were dug in just a few feet from the edge of the road, stubbornly still firing despite the rising torrent of gunfire the Americans were bringing to bear against them.

One of the enemy soldiers took a bullet in his face and fell back in the grassy undergrowth. Another North Korean was shot in the arm; cut down by a scything sweep of gunfire from one of the M240s.

Gillette gathered a handful of men around him behind the steel shelter of his command vehicle in the middle of the convoy. His eyes were glazed over with unholy rage, his head hunched low on his shoulders like a boxer ready to brawl.

"We're going to rush the fuckers!" he decided. "We hit them with grenades, and then we go in after them."

The men gathered themselves, tensing their bodies like coiled springs, ready for the order that might mean their deaths. Gillette guessed the North Koreans were about fifty paces further down the slope. It was a long throw for a grenade, but he gave the order regardless, hoping the dust and the percussive noise of the explosions would give his men the distraction they needed to close and kill.

"Grenades!"

Three riflemen rose from behind the Oshkosh and pitched grenades. Two pounding heartbeats later the munitions exploded, flinging great gouts of dirt and rock into the air, blanketing the roadside in swirling dust.

"Come on! Follow me!" Gillette sprang to his feet, firing from the hip as he charged headlong down the dirt road. An enemy round struck him flush in the chest but was deflected by his IOTV body armor.

His men ran with him, teeth clenched, tensed but their discipline overriding their terror. They burst through the dust haze and found the enemy soldiers in a small knot, camouflaged amongst a clump of roadside trees and gnarled roots. Gillette broke through the undergrowth, growling like an animal. He went for the North Koreans, roaring and clubbing and firing in a murderous frenzy from close range. One enemy combatant was dead, another two were wounded, and there was one other raggedly dressed enemy soldier, dazed and disoriented cowering in the bottom of a shallow firing pit. The stunned enemy soldier fumbled with his weapon and tried to swing the barrel onto Gillette, then saw the dreadful savagery in the American officer's face and faltered. He threw up his hands in surrender, pale-faced and gaunt. The rest of the Americans swept onwards down the slope, beating at the bushes, spraying the forest's fringe with fire to ensure the road was clear of other ambushers, leaving Gillette and the remaining North Korean alone. The North Korean soldier's eyes filled with tears of humiliation, and he began to weep. He said something which might have been a desperate appeal, or perhaps a vile curse.

Gillette did not know – or care.

He emptied his magazine into the North Korean's chest, his features set into a merciless executioner's mask.

*

The battle-scarred and blood-spattered M-ATVs at the vanguard of the convoy lumbered and swayed through the canopy of shadow-struck forest and finally burst into a bright sunlit compound of beaten earth. The trucks transporting the injured troops braked to a halt and Gillette clambered down out of his command Oshkosh with a look of mild astonishment on his face, tempered by his urgent responsibility to get medical attention for his wounded.

The clearing was almost a square mile in size; the ground bulldozed of trees and the fallen logs piled high at the eastern perimeter to form a defensive wall. Close to the trees were great mounds of bridging equipment and a handful of heavy vehicles. At the southern edge of the clearing stood a dozen tents that housed troops from the 14th Brigade Engineer Battalion, their distinctive coat of arms fluttering from a small flag atop the largest tent. Crewmen stopped their work as the trucks pulled into view and gaped at the troops of Alpha Company as they disembarked their transports.

Tonneguzzi came forward and paused next to Gillette but had no time to share his captain's bemused wonder at their new surroundings.

"Medics! Medics!" the XO cast a desperate glance around the compound, his eyes searching the mind-boggling array of tents and equipment. "Medics!"

In response to the XO's frantic plea, a handful of men came running from an aid station close to the northern edge of the clearing. They dashed towards the trucks and Tonneguzzi ran forward to intercept them.

"We've got two dead and five wounded," he seized one of the running men by the arm and explained breathlessly, reporting only what was essential and necessary. "They're in the rear truck. Bullet wounds and shrapnel injuries."

The team of camp medics were led by a grey-haired officer with the kindly face of a school teacher. He clambered up into the back of the truck and quickly took command, snapping orders as he stepped amongst the bloody wounded, assessing each one with the quick, incisive experience of an ER specialist.

Tonneguzzi and Alpha Company's own exhausted medics stayed by the truck until all of the wounded men had been carried on litters to the aid station on the far side of the camp. The XO was fraught with fatigue and made haggard by trauma. His steps were leaden with exhaustion by the time he joined Gillette, who stood waiting by the open door of his Oshkosh.

"How bad is it?" Gillette read his XO's distressed expression and gruffed the question.

Tonneguzzi shrugged, his features rumpled and working with the depths of his despair. "Bates might not make it," he said with quiet concern. "They're going to have to rip his chest open to operate. The doc says he's fifty-fifty. Miguel Gonzalez might lose his leg."

"Fuck!" Gillette grimaced, anguished and angry, his mind flashing back to the first frantic moments the North Koreans had attacked. He asked himself again, for the hundredth time, if he could have done anything to anticipate the enemy attack – but he had dutifully exercised every precaution. The ambushers had been suicidal fanatics, committed to their cause and resigned to their own certain death.

"Detail some men to hose the blood from the trucks," Gillette said.

Tonneguzzi grunted to conceal a twinge of bitter resentment and studied the granite-like set of Gillette's hard face. Two good riflemen were dead, and several others had been injured – and instead of grieving compassion, Gillette's compulsive priority was to make sure the vehicles were washed down and all evidence of the attack scrubbed away. "I'll see to it," he said tightly.

A swarthy man with his uniform sleeves rolled up to his bulging forearms appeared from the engineering command tent. He was a tall, rangy figure with an anvil jaw and short dark hair. His face was weather-beaten, and his hands were the size of baseball mitts. He strode purposefully towards Gillette and Tonneguzzi.

"Captain Leroy Fawkes," he stepped up to Gillette and thrust out his hand. The two men shook. "14th Brigade Engineer Battalion based out of Lewis-McChord, Washington," the man introduced himself, then peered with macabre dismay at the bullet-riddled convoy of vehicles and the rivulets of blood that streaked the transport trucks.

"Captain Buck Gillette, Alpha Company, 3rd Battalion," Gillette was struck by the intensity of the engineer officer's eyes. "And this is my XO, Lieutenant Mario Tonneguzzi."

Fawkes stepped back, propped his hands on his hips and inspected the bedraggled column of vehicles with a grave expression. "You boys run into trouble along the way?"

"An ambush," Gillette said succinctly. "Suicidal North Koreans still devoted to the memory of their Dear Leader."

"Fuckers," Captain Fawkes spat. "These mountains are full of them. They're like fucking vermin. Did you kill them all?"

"Yes."

"But we lost two good men and five more were wounded," Tonneguzzi interjected.

"Fuckers!" Fawkes grimaced and then fell silent for a long somber moment before he seemed to shrug off the grim news with a resigned sigh. Death and injury were an inevitable consequence of war. Eventually even the most benevolent men became hardened to the harsh reality. With a visible effort Fawkes' expression changed and his tone became matter-of-fact.

"Well, welcome to Camp WOFTAM," he said more formally. "I wish it was in better circumstances." WOFTAM was a military slang acronym for 'waste of fucking time and money'. "I don't know what mission you boys are on, but someone in Division thinks it's mighty important."

Gillette blinked. The vast compound and the piles of heavy equipment certainly suggested an operation far more significant than he had anticipated. He had spent the entire morning rueing that Alpha Company had been pulled out of Dandong for some minor reconnaissance patrol in the middle of the Chinese forest. Now he felt a lift of renewed optimism.

Fawkes pointed out the arrangement of tents and the equipment that had been assembled. "The rest of your battalion are due later tonight. In the meantime, there's hot chow waiting in the mess for your boys, and your guests have set themselves up the northeast corner. You might want to get acquainted."

"Guests?" Gillette frowned.

"A platoon of 4th Rangers, British Army," the Engineer officer looked a little puzzled by Gillette's confused expression. "They've set up camp in some of your tents. They've been here since yesterday, preparing for the mission. Didn't your commanding officer tell you this was a joint op?"

*

Gillette's already disgruntled mood turned thunderously sour in an instant. He barked at the company to finish disembarking the transports, then turned to Tonneguzzi, still scowling with hateful intent.

"Mario, get these vehicles washed down, then go and make sure the men are settled. Once the boys are chowing down and resting, I want you at the aid station with our wounded."

"Okay," the XO said obediently. "Where will you be?"

"I'm going to deliver a verbal eviction notice to our unwelcome British squatters," Gillette's tone dripped with ominous threat.

The platoon of British Rangers had set up camp in a handful of tents that engineers had erected for Alpha Company troops. Gillette turned and stared at the allied soldiers from a distance. They seemed totally oblivious to the arrival of the Americans; moving about the encampment with introverted focus on their tasks. Most of the British soldiers were cleaning their weapons and checking through their combat kits. A few slept in the sun. Others sat close together, talking quietly amongst themselves and drinking from tin cups.

Seething with irrational indignation, Gillette strode purposefully towards the British.

"You men will have to relocate to another part of the compound," he declared loudly from halfway across the clearing, gesturing with a wave of his arm.

One of the British soldiers looked up, peered laconically at Gillette, and then went back to stripping down his weapon, unperturbed.

"Did you hear me?" Gillette's loud commanding voice boomed. The British seemed singularly unimpressed. They were small-framed lean men with dark eyes and serious faces who moved with subdued economy – very different to the loud, brash swagger of the Americans.

As Gillette approached the knot of tents, a compact man with dark straight hair and a sun browned face emerged from the shadows. He carried himself with an air of quiet authority and held a tin of steaming tea in one hand. He had dark, intelligent eyes and a quizzical expression on his face.

"Who are you?" the man asked, then sipped casually from his mug. He wore the uniform of a British lieutenant.

"Who the fuck are you?" Gillette shot back.

The British officer seemed unfazed by Gillette's bluster, and unbothered by the larger man's bulking muscled approach. He stood his ground calmly, his voice never rising.

"Lieutenant Michael Loftus," the Englishman introduced himself. He stood no taller than Gillette's chin. He made no move to shake hands. "The lads call me 'Lofty'. 4th Rangers, British Army."

"Well, I'm Captain Buck Gillette, Alpha Company 3rd Battalion, 15th god-damned Infantry regiment – and your squad of men are camped in tents that have been set aside for my soldiers."

"Is that it?" the Englishman mocked Gillette with a bemused smile. "You're pissed off and spewing lava because we've commandeered a couple of your tents? It's hardly an offense punishable by execution."

"I don't give a shit what you think," Gillette's temper reached the end of its fuse. "My troops are fighting men who have just come off the battlefront at Dandong city. They need rest, and there ain't no way I'm going to compromise their well-being for a handful of fucking British REMFS who want to pretend they're real soldiers."

REMF was derogatory American military slang for 'rear echelon mother fucker'. The British officer understood the reference and smiled a lazy taunting smile, still calm and composed, unruffled by the big American's bluster. A couple of the Rangers who had been sitting, quietly drinking, got slowly to their feet. Gillette caught the movement from the corner of his eye but stood his ground defiantly. For Gillette this sleight seemed the final ignominy. After being criticized instead of lauded for his tactical ambush of the Chinese armored column, and then being abruptly pulled off the front line and shunted twenty miles away from the fighting for some anonymous incursion across the border, now his men's accommodation had been seconded by British troops who had probably never seen combat.

"We're not moving, old boy," the British officer provoked Gillette with an upper-class English expression, his face still relaxed but his eyes glinting like a knife in the shadows.

Gillette hesitated for just a heartbeat. The British officer lolled indolently against the post of a tent and smiled again. This time Gillette saw the mocking defiance in the other man's eyes more plainly. He had judged these allied troops as foppish raw recruits, new to the war, but he had been wrong. There was something wolfish in the Englishman's eyes that reflected the dark experiences of combat's horror.

Tonneguzzi, as always, timed his arrival perfectly. The XO was accustomed to Gillette's abrasive gung-ho manner and the size of his captain's ego. He appeared at Gillette's shoulder, conciliatory and calming. He flicked a glance at the British officer, and then got Gillette's attention.

"The men are all bunked down," he said matter-of-factly. "Everyone has headed off to the mess tent. The leadership group are waiting for you to deliver another warno (warning order), and Lieutenant Colonel Reilly has been on comms. He wants to speak with you."

Gillette grunted, still glowering at the British lieutenant who had so effortlessly defied him. Gillette's fists were bunched, his body tense as an animal straining at the leash, hackles bristling. Then slowly, he relaxed, though malevolence still blazed brightly in his eyes.

"I reckon you and I will just have to find another time to air our grievances," he threatened. The British Ranger saluted Gillette with a mocking tip of his tin mug. "Drop by any time, old chap," he emphasized the lazy inflection of his accent. "We're always willing to have a friendly little chat with our gallant American counterparts."

*

Sudden commotion and the sound of revving engines announced the arrival of the remainder of 3rd Battalion two hours after dusk. The trucks arrived in darkness, their military blackout lights glowing against the falling night.

Within an hour of arrival, Lieutenant Colonel Reilly summonsed Gillette to his headquarters tent.

The tent was still a disordered chaos of equipment, radio gear and maps. A desk and a chair stood in the middle of the space, but there was no other furniture, no sense of permanency. Gillette ducked beneath the canvas flap and stood at attention until Reilly made the effort to notice him.

The battalion commander appeared distracted, rifling through sheafs of bundled paper until he found the information he wanted. Without any preamble or social pleasantries, he launched into his briefing.

"Alpha Company will be moving out tonight at 2300 hours," Reilly began and gestured at a map rolled open on his desktop beneath the scatter of paperwork. He pointed then spread his hands like a wizard casting a spell. "The engineers will erect a bailey bridge directly north of our position. You and your men will cross the Yalu and push into enemy territory. The ground is densely forested. Three miles north east of the crossing point is a battery of eight Chinese PLZ-05 self-propelled howitzers," Reilly pressed his thumb down on an area of the map and Gillette dutifully crossed to the desk to study the terrain more carefully. The forest location was at the end of a dirt road that seemed to run away into the woods and then stop abruptly. Beneath the map lay a series of grainy spy satellite images. Reilly rearranged everything on his desk to reveal the photos.

Gillette leaned closer. He could see the dirt road and the eight Chinese artillery pieces. They appeared each to be standing hull-down within revetted gun emplacements. Backed up against the wall of woods that surrounded the site he could also clearly see an encampment of several rows of tents.

"The Chinese howitzers are in a clearing the enemy have bulldozed," Reilly went on. "And Allied command wants the weapons destroyed before we make a push into the heart of

Dandong. From their current position these long-range Chinese artillery pieces are a clear and dangerous threat to our advance."

Gillette grunted. It was a shit mission.

"Why can't a handful of our fighter jets just take them out?" he argued. "A couple of F-16's could do the job."

"Because the ingress approaches to the target are bristling with Chinese air-defense missiles," Reilly answered with ire, like he had expected the question.

"What about drones?" Gillette persisted, "or counter battery fire from our own long-range guns?"

"We can't use drones," Reilly flicked an irritated sideways glance at Gillette. The battalion commander's face was grim. "The Chinese have deployed hand-held anti-drone devices similar to the Dronebusters our own army have been testing in Europe. Any drone we send towards the site would be jammed. The only way to take those howitzers out is a surprise ground attack by infantry armed with Javelins."

Gillette sighed and looked blank. It wasn't the mission he had hoped for. There was no glory in knocking out a battery of howitzers miles from anywhere.

It was a shit mission.

Reilly sensed Gillette's disgruntled apathy but cared not in the slightest for his captain's attitude. "Do not commit your men to close-quarters combat with the artillery crews. Stay within the fringe of the woods. The crews that service these weapons do not matter – it's the howitzers that must be destroyed. Once all the guns are knocked out, you will withdraw back to the bridge." He went on remorselessly. "You will be escorted to the site by a platoon of British Rangers under the command of Lieutenant Loftus. His men will guide you to the attack point."

It was the final ignominy for Gillette and the blank expression on his face turned belligerent.

"With all due respect, sir," he growled through gritted teeth, "me and my men don't need a tour guide to reach a combat objective. Just give us a map and a compass. We're not girl guides – we're elite US Army soldiers."

Reilly flinched and then his face tightened, his eyes flashing bright with sudden temper. "Captain Gillette, you seem to be under the mistaken impression that I have called you here to request your cooperation," the senior officer's voice rose as he punched out the words. "You are wrong. I called you here to issue orders. They are not negotiable, nor is your opinion wanted."

Gillette fought back an impulsive expletive and pressed his lips tight into a thin pale line. Reilly looked towards the tent flap and nodded imperceptibly. A moment later Lieutenant Loftus ambled into the tent and stood at ease beside Gillette.

"I understand you two men have met," Reilly smiled at the Ranger without humor. "So that saves the time to make introductions," he turned and glared at Gillette for a long disapproving moment, then proceeded with an explanation. "Captain Gillette, the Brit boys have been conducting covert surveillance on the north side of the Yalu for the past three weeks. They know the terrain intimately. They will escort Alpha Company to the Chinese battery park where you will launch an attack from within the woods at precisely 0400 hours tomorrow morning. Are my orders clear?"

"Yes, sir," Gillette snapped through a red mist of temper.

"Good," Reilly signaled that the briefing was over. "Then make your preparations, get your kit, equipment and men together, and be ready to move out at 2300 hours. Dismissed."

*

Once outside the HQ tent, Gillette paused for a bitter moment of fuming resentment. He threw his head back, straining with anger, and then heard the canvas tent flap rustle behind him. An instant later Lieutenant Loftus appeared at his shoulder. Casually, the British officer lit a cigarette and inhaled deeply.

Gillette turned savagely on the Ranger and flashed a murderous glance.

"I don't trust allied troops," Gillette snarled. "You're all soft REMFs who like to play at soldier, but never get in the fight, so hear me out you Limey bastard," he thrust a menacing fist in the Englishman's face. "When we get to that attack point, you stay the fuck out of my way. Fighting is for real men. Let my boys handle the Chinese howitzers. I don't want to be tripping over your candy-ass pretenders when the bullets start flying."

Lieutenant Loftus said nothing.

Chapter 5:

Gillette returned to his encamped troops and spoke heatedly to Tonneguzzi for several minutes before issuing another warning order to the unit's leadership group. He made no effort to veil his seething bitterness.

"We're moving out at 2300 hours and heading north into enemy territory. The fuckin' Brits are going to guide us to a battery of Chinese long-range self-propelled howitzers. We attack at precisely 0400 hours tomorrow and we take the guns out with Javelins," he brusquely recited the essentials, then left Tonneguzzi to arrange the details and fend off questions.

The troops marched from the encampment at zero hour. By the time the column reached the banks of the Yalu, the engineers were just completing the assembly of the ribbon bridge.

The British Rangers led the way across the river with the men of Alpha Company following in loose files.

Heavy rain clouds had swept in from the west throughout the evening and now they hung low over the forest, holding in the heat of the afternoon so that the men were lathered with sweat. Then the rain came; soft pattering droplets that dripped through the canopy of foliage and swept amongst the trees in pearlescent veils of mist. The darkness closed in around them, so complete that it became disorientating, and every errant sound seemed amplified. Progress slowed to a faltering shuffle and men cursed bitterly under their breath as the dirt beneath their feet turned glutinous with mud.

Gillette marched at the head of the Americans with the platoon of Rangers single-filed in front of him. Every man was equipped with ENVG-B goggles to reveal the route forward, yet still many walked with one hand on the shoulder of the man in front of him, so the entire column seemed like a serpentining conga line as it snaked through the pitch blackness. Gillette could hear the hissed grumbles of the men when they lost their footing and the incessant small sounds of equipment rattling. Every step towards danger seemed to ratchet up the tension.

The sounds of the forest were masked by the intermittent patter of the rain and several times the column stopped for no apparent reason, each man suddenly forced to stand perfectly still on heightened alert until the 'all clear' was whispered from ear to ear and progress resumed.

The earthy smells of the surrounding forest seemed amplified and once Gillette thought he smelled woodsmoke somewhere in the distance. More prominent was the sweaty scent of nervous anxiety that permeated the men's skin and drifted in whiffs on the heavy air that closed tight about them.

The ground beneath the men's feet began to slowly incline and then they were leaning forward against the slope of a hill, trudging under the weight of their equipment and beginning to strain from the rising tension and physical effort. Gillette could hear the rasp of the men's breathing and then someone slipped and swore. A sergeant somewhere further down the line hissed angrily and the sound was abruptly cut off.

They reached the crest of the rise, and the column shuffled to yet another interminable halt. Gillette stood docile and impatient, seething silently at the delay. The rain stopped abruptly, and a zephyr of cool breeze brushed through the treetops. He glanced up through the forest canopy and glimpsed patches of clear night sky and twinkling stars. Then a serious dark face ghosted out of the night, just a few inches from his own.

"Chinese patrol," Lieutenant Loftus breathed. "They're somewhere ahead of us. Pass the word to the rest of your men to lay down."

Gillette turned slowly and leaned towards the man trailing him. "Enemy patrol. Lie down. Pass the word."

Gillette sank to his haunches and waited, his finger curled around the trigger of his M4, his goggled eyes scanning the wall of trees that pressed in around him from every direction. He stole a glance at his wristwatch and cursed the delay.

A quarter of an hour passed; fifteen torturous minutes of tension and straining. His mouth felt dry, his heart thumping within the cage of his chest.

"If the enemy stumble onto us right now, I'll lose half the company and the mission will be a disaster," Gillette's thoughts raced, fear and anxiety torturing his state of mind. Somewhere to the north there was a flash of light in the sky followed by the echo of rumbling thunder. A dull red glow lit the belly of the clouds for just a heartbeat. Gillette understood instinctively; one of the Chinese howitzers had fired to announce a new dawning day of death and destruction.

He saw the figure approaching from the head of the column through his goggles and he rose slowly to his feet. Lieutenant Loftus breathed in his ear. "All clear, but we're behind time. Tell your men to keep up. I'll not wait for anyone who can't handle the pace."

The ungainly column moved forward again, wending their way down the face of the hill, back down to the dense forest floor. The ground levelled out and the men became intuitively infected with a rising sense of urgency and impatience. Another Chinese howitzer fired and this time the sound of the great gun's wicked retort seemed much closer. A flare of dull orange light flashed through the palisade of trees and then faded.

A breath of chill wind filtered through the forest and carried with it the pungent aroma of smoke.

At last, the column stopped, and the British Rangers seemed to melt away into the surrounding woods until only Lieutenant Loftus remained. Gillette shuffled forward. The darkness was no longer absolute. Eerie pre-dawn light filtered through the trees. He and the British lieutenant stood close together.

"The enemy guns are fifty yards directly ahead," the Englishman pointed. As if to confirm the proximity of the Chinese artillery park, another great howitzer fired and this time the ghastly roar of the great gun echoed loud and clear, and the earth trembled.

The British and American troops went to ground, each man with their weapons at the ready, their senses heightened and alert for errant sounds that might signal another enemy patrol or a tell-tale sign of a waiting ambush.

Gillette went forward, creeping like a thief, with the British officer at his shoulder. He reached the fringe of the woods and crouched low, hidden in shadows. Stealth was not necessary. The Chinese howitzers had suddenly begun to fire in concert, one gun after the other cracking the pre-dawn sky apart with the thunder of their roar. The fiery orange blast of each launched round lit the clearing up in a semaphore of vivid flashes of light, painting the entire landscape with a flickering garish orange glow.

Gillette watched each of the eight self-propelled howitzers fire. From where he crouched, hidden, the enemy guns were in a diagonal echelon, running away from him; the closest perhaps just a couple of hundred yards distant, the furthest about a mile away. Each howitzer was serviced by a bustling crew of Chinese gunners; tiny black silhouettes against the flash and blast, industrious as ants.

Gillette took a long moment to study the terrain before deciding his dispositions. Mario Tonneguzzi crept forward and joined the two men. Gillette acknowledged his XO with a grunt, then pointed. "We use First and Second platoon to form a firing line," he said, "And we'll hold the remnants of Third platoon back as a reserve with the HQ element. Tell Lieutenant Geyer to set up his mortars, and I want the Javelins in good firing positions and in deep cover. I want them to target the furthest away howitzers first."

Tonneguzzi nodded and crept back into the forest to oversee the troop dispositions. Gillette turned to Lieutenant Loftus. "I want your Ranger platoon to sweep east to where the enemy tents are pitched. Once my boys open fire on the howitzers, I want your men to pour fire into the Chinese gun crews and their tents. Understand?"

Lieutenant Loftus frowned, then smiled with a look of dawning bemusement. The corners of his eyebrows raised and his brow furrowed, giving the English officer's face a look of satanical malevolence. His lips drew back tight, revealing his bared teeth.

"My men are not under your command, Captain Gillette, and this is not our fight, not our mission," the British Ranger said flatly. "We have followed our orders. The attack on the Chinese howitzers is up to you to execute."

"*What?*" Gillette's eyes narrowed, his temper rising with a sudden sense of astonishment, but it felt like treachery.

The Englishman went on matter-of-factly. "Our orders were to escort you to the enemy gun emplacements. That's all."

Gillette's temper flared brighter than the flash of a Chinese howitzer firing. "You gutless, spineless cowards!" he croaked the accusation; his expression monstrous with loathing.

Loftus seemed completely unfazed by Gillette's violent outburst. The British officer's smile turned villainous with relish. "We have our own orders. Our role in this attack is done. We're leaving. Good luck."

"I knew you REMF Brit bastards weren't real warriors!" Gillette hissed a parting salvo.

The retreating Englishman never faltered in step. Instead, he glanced briefly over his shoulder.

"0400 hours That's the time you attack. Don't forget."

*

Mario Tonneguzzi looked concerned and bewildered. He broke the news to Gillette like a doctor delivering a fatal diagnosis, grimacing as he spoke.

"The Brit officer was right, Buck," the XO spoke in the soothing voice a parent uses on a petulant child. "The Rangers were never ordered to take part in the attack. This is an Alpha Company mission."

Gillette glowered. He cast his mind back to the briefing with Reilly and annoyingly could not specifically recall the battalion commander making any mention of the British Rangers being part of the assault on the howitzers.

He had simply assumed...

"Damn!" he spat, and then spewed a torrent of vile expletives. Somehow, his own oversight only served to further enhance his loathing of all allied troops. He sat, fuming in the still darkness, until he had control of his temper, and then forced himself to re-think the attack.

He shook his head like a boxer trying to shrug off the effects of a crunching blow to the jaw and his senses began to clear.

He glanced at his wristwatch. It was 0230 hours. He leaned close to his XO.

"Okay, we will keep the FIST team and headquarters element where they are, behind First and Second platoon. The remnants of Third platoon will have to join the fight," he decided. "I'm going to lead them around the perimeter of the clearing and position them close to the enemy tents. While I'm gone, I want the rest of our boys dug in – and I want a handful of men with each of the Javelins for close-weapons support in case the Chinese try to mount some kind of counter-attack. Understand?"

Tonneguzzi nodded, but Gillette went on, emphasizing the point. "Those Javelins must be protected at all costs until every howitzer is destroyed."

"Got it," Tonneguzzi nodded.

Gillette gathered the men of 3rd Platoon around him in the darkness of the forest and explained his intentions. Some of the faces that peered back at him in the oppressive gloom were strangers; new recruits who had been shunted into the unit less than twenty-four hours ago to replace the men killed and wounded during the ambush on the streets of Dandong. The new platoon sergeant was a tall man with a scarred face, fresh off a transport plane from Camp Humphreys.

"We're heading out," Gillette explained. "On the east side of the enemy compound there is an encampment of enemy artillery crew tents. That's our objective. Once we locate a suitable firing position you are going to go to ground and find good cover."

The troops reached for their gear and Gillette drew the platoon lieutenant and his new sergeant aside.

"When you see the first Javelins strike, you open fire on the tents in the compound and kill every Chinese artillery crewman you see."

Though it was still oppressively dark in the dense tangle of forest, Gillette went forward confidently, keeping the perimeter of the compound visible over his left shoulder through the wall of trees. The ground was level, though dense with knee-high grass, bushes and fallen logs.

Despite the orange glow of artillery fire that lit the fringes of the forest and the muffling thunder of each shot being fired, Gillette still exercised caution, wary of enemy patrols. Behind him the men of 3rd Platoon trudged stoically, sweating and tense until Gillette called a sudden halt. The platoon sank to their haunches and Gillette went forward with the lieutenant at his shoulder. They crept to the fringe of the trees and peered through the thinning veil of foliage.

"Here," Gillette whispered, and gestured with his hands where he wanted the platoon to deploy. The two men were concealed in scruffy foliage about five yards inside the edge of the woods. Across the clearing they could see at least a dozen large Chinese tents, each of them hidden under camouflage netting. The closest tent was perhaps just a hundred yards away, an eerily silent shape cloaked in shadows.

Gillette figured the Chinese gun crews who were not working the howitzers would be resting in shifts. He had no idea how many men serviced a battery of Chinese self-propelled guns, but he guessed a hundred or more, including support and maintenance staff. Lieutenant Colonel Reilly had warned him at their briefing that only the howitzers mattered – but the opportunity to slaughter so many experienced enemy artillerymen was an opportunity too tempting for Gillette to ignore.

"Remember," he whispered to the platoon lieutenant. "You don't open fire until the first howitzer goes up in flames. That will be your signal to hit them with everything you've got."

*

When Gillette returned to where First and Second platoons were preparing their positions, he found Tonneguzzi knee deep in a shallow ditch, surveying the field of fire for one of the Javelin teams. The XO looked up and recognized Gillette's silhouette, backlit by a flash of Chinese howitzer fire. Tonneguzzi had his sleeves rolled up and his face was smeared with grime and sweat. Like the rest of the troops, he had worked at a frenzied pace in Gillette's absence to ensure each man would shoot from good cover. He climbed out of the shallow ditch and dusted himself off. Gillette glanced at his watch. He had been away for almost an hour.

"It's 0330," he grunted, then watched the two-man Javelin team settle themselves into place and sort through their weapon reloads. "SITREP."

"Everyone is in place," the two officers stood close together as the XO delivered his report. "The mortars are set up a hundred yards to our rear and both platoons are in position," Tonneguzzi explained in a whisper, though caution seemed hardly necessary. The Chinese howitzers were in full roar and, overhead, hidden by the night and the clouds, the scream of allied fighter jet engines could be heard, echoing across the sky as they flew northwards on dawn combat missions.

Together Gillette and Tonneguzzi crept through the fringe of the woods, moving from man to man, inspecting each firing position. The soldiers were spread out in a long line with the two Javelins at the western end from where they had clear views of the Chinese guns, and the two M240 machine guns positioned at the eastern end of the line, closest to the encampment of enemy tents. Gillette could find no faults. Some of the riflemen had piled loose stones about them, others had found convenient fallen tree trunks for shelter. Gillette completed his inspection and let out a tight breath.

He took up position in the center of the line, sharing a hollow of overgrown ground with Tonneguzzi and his RTO. He checked his watch again, then reached for a pair of binoculars and slowly surveyed the Chinese compound. The enemy howitzers had worked themselves up into a relentless fury, firing one after the other and, no doubt, bombarding important allied targets around the outskirts of Dandong. The sound of their salvos became an unending thunderclap of violent noise and lightning strikes of flashing fire. Dust drifted across the clearing in shifting clouds as each weapon recoiled on its massive steel tracks. He dropped the glasses to rest his eyes, and a few moments later heard Tonneguzzi take a short sharp breath of surprise.

"The Chinese artillery has stopped," the XO breathed and pointed.

The heavy silence in the aftermath of the enemy's pre-dawn bombardment seemed eerie with foreboding. Gillette snatched for the binoculars again and peered hard. For a long moment he said nothing, and then suddenly understanding began to dawn.

"They're changing gun crews," he said with a rasp of disbelief in his throat, still doubting his eyes. The enemy artillery park was suddenly veiled in gloom. It was not the pitch black of night but the peculiar glow of twilight; that obscure filtered light that rims the horizon before the dawn. Against that ghostly backdrop the Chinese artillery crews seemed to be filing to and from the rows of compound tents.

"They might be changing fire missions, or perhaps they're re-supplying the guns with more ammunition," Tonneguzzi reasoned.

Gillette shrugged. It didn't matter. The fact was that he had been presented with a heaven-sent opportunity to seize the tactical advantage.

He cast aside the binoculars and thought fast. He glanced at his watch, suddenly infected with a rush of fevered agitation.

It was 0345 hours. Gillette made a tight face, his eyes alight with cruel savagery, his mind making the calculations. Tonneguzzi recognized the reckless rashness in his captain's face and felt a sick slide of disquiet turn his guts into tight knots. "Buck, what in the hell are you thinking?"

Gillette's eyes turned hard as stone. "I'm thinking we should attack right now," he said. "While we have the advantage."

"Now?" Tonneguzzi could not disguise his appalled reaction. "We have orders to wait until 0400."

"I know."

"And if we wait, we will still have the element of surprise."

"But not the cover of darkness," Gillette reasoned.

"But still –"

"But nothing," Gillette's imagination raced ahead, his mind calculating risk and reward. He could see the chaos and confusion an attack in the dark would create through the Chinese gun crews. The Americans were all wearing their ENVG-B goggles. The augmented reality binoculars would turn the Chinese artillery teams into sitting ducks for his riflemen and machine gunners while the Americans remained largely invisible. He could storm the compound and his troops could run amok, slaughtering enemy combatants at will. If he waited until the howitzers resumed their fire, the flash and flare of the enemy guns would light his men up and give the Chinese a chance to fight back.

"Buck, we have orders," the XO insisted.

"But now we have opportunity," Gillette countered. "I thought those cowardly Brit fuckers were going to join the fight. I was counting on their firepower to help hold off any organized enemy resistance. Okay, that was my error," he grudgingly conceded, "but now we have another tactical element we can use to our advantage. After we destroy the howitzers, we can storm the compound and kill every one of those Chinese bastards."

"Buck," Tonneguzzi tried to reason with his captain, sensing Gillette was on the verge of a catastrophic error. "We don't have orders to attack the compound. Our instructions were to destroy the Chinese howitzers and then withdraw back to the bridge. The artillery crews don't matter if the PLZ-05s are knocked out. Killing the crews is not the mission priority."

"My job is to win the war," Gillette's voice took on an edge of menace. "And that means killing every fucker wearing an enemy uniform. Generals, infantrymen and fucking artillery crews."

"Our job is to destroy the guns," Tonneguzzi retorted. "That's all we were ordered to do. It's why we dug in, for Christ's sake – so we could pour fire into the enemy from good cover, and then withdraw safely."

Gillette fell silent for a heartbeat and Tonneguzzi dared to hope that his captain had suddenly seen reason.

Beyond their firing position the Chinese artillery park was still shrouded in eerie darkness, the big howitzers silent silhouettes against the ghostly pre-dawn light. But when Gillette spoke again, his voice was firm and resolved.

"We're going to attack – now."

"Buck, Lieutenant Colonel Reilly's orders were specific. The attack has been planned for 0400 hours."

"If we wait, we will lose the advantage of darkness," Gillette bit back stubbornly.

"Then at least get Reilly on comms before you make up your mind. Explain the situation to HQ before you make a rash decision."

"There's no time!" Gillette snarled. "The Chinese guns could recommence firing at any moment."

Tonneguzzi shook his head and for an instant Gillette thought his XO was on the verge of mutiny. "What about the bigger picture?" the XO pleaded. "What if there's some rationale behind the designated 0400 attack time?"

"What bigger picture?" Gillette growled. "*We are the only fucking picture.* Brigade brought Alpha Company here because we're the best fucking unit in the army. They shipped us out of Dandong to do a job that they didn't trust anyone else to do."

"And what about the Brits?"

"What about them?" Gillette's fury sparked. "They surveiled the site and located the guns. They guided us to the attack point because they're not the kind of fighting men we are. By now those useless Limey bastards are probably back in *our* god-damned tents sleeping or sipping on cups of hot fucking tea."

Tonneguzzi sat back on his haunches, his expression aghast, slowly shaking his head in dismay. "Remember the ass-chewing Reilly gave you for the ambush?" he spoke softly, placatingly. "That was the same scenario, Buck. You took it upon yourself to ignore orders because a tactical advantage presented itself. You took a massive risk, and men got killed and wounded as a result of that decision."

"Yes," Gillette said without a hint of remorse. "But I was right, dammit. We knocked out a handful of enemy tanks and APCs, and slaughtered close to a full company of Chinese troops. We also averted an imminent attack on our position. Why?" Gillette snarled. "I'll tell you why. Because I had the guts and the instincts to see the threat and find a way to avert it. It was me, Mario. Me. If I'd called up battalion and waited for them to decide, we might *all* be dead right now."

Tonneguzzi said nothing. He had the sense that Gillette was already committed to an attack, despite his objections. Instead, he studied Gillette's face; watched the man's expressions change as he wrestled with a decision that had life and death consequences.

In a last desperate bid to avert an impulsive attack, the XO said quietly, "We won't have a numerical advantage. We don't have overwhelming numbers. If a handful of the Chinese put up a fight…"

Gillette shook his head. "They won't stand," he said emphatically.

"How can you be sure? What if you're wrong?"

"I'm not wrong," Gillette thrust out his chin in arrogant disdain. "They're just fucking Chinese gun crews. They probably haven't fired a small arm since they completed basic training. And we're Alpha Company. We're the best fucking unit in this man's army. We're the elite."

Tonneguzzi held his breath and glanced past the fringe of trees towards the clearing. The pre-dawn light seemed a little brighter than it had been just a few minutes earlier. He could make out the shapes of soldiers marching across the compound like a trail of ants, moving towards the silent bulk of the waiting howitzers. In another minute he sensed the Chinese guns would recommence their deadly barrage.

Gillette turned to his RTO. "Get me on the company net, pronto," he snapped irritably.

The RTO opened a line and Gillette spoke quickly and urgently to the three platoon leaders. "We are attacking in thirty seconds!"

He tossed the handset back to the RTO.

The decision was made.

There was no time to consider his choice, no time for second-guessing. Vacillating was a sign of weak leadership, he knew. Warriors were decisive.

"Stay here and open fire as soon as the first howitzer explodes," he told Tonneguzzi. "I'm going to alert the Javelin teams and supervise their first shots."

Mario Tonneguzzi made a forlorn shrug of grudging acquiescence but said nothing.

*

Gillette sprinted for the western end of the line where the two Javelins were situated, bounding through the undergrowth like a rabbit flushed from cover, jinking and weaving around obstacles, stumbling when he lost his footing. He reached the closest Javelin team and hissed his orders without slowing.

"Fire! Fire now! Go! Go! Go!"

Startled by the urgency of the command, the two crewmen who operated the FGM-148 leaped abruptly to their work, loading the anti-tank weapon with a warhead and going through the process of selecting their target.

Gillette ran on. The second Javelin emplacement was at the far end of the line. When he reached the shallow scrape of ground, he was dripping sweat, his breath sawing across his throat.

"Open fire!" he snapped.

The weapons operator obediently hefted the CLU to his shoulder and powered up the unit. The instant the battery hummed to life, the loader forced a missile into the launch tube and slapped the weapon's operator on the shoulder. The operator dropped to a kneeling position with his left leg braced forward, taking his body weight onto his right knee and targeted the most distant Chinese howitzer. The weapon's sensors picked up the vehicle's infrared signature. The operator selected 'top attack' and then felt for the fire trigger with his finger.

Buck Gillette growled. "Hit the bastards hard!"

The Javelin was a 'fire-and-forget' weapon that used an imaging infrared system to lock onto enemy tanks at distances up to five thousand yards. The operator took a last long breath to compose himself, then squeezed the trigger.

The CLU punched hard into the operator's shoulder and the Javelin missile was ejected from the launch tube. After a split-second of delay the missile's flight motor ignited on a feather of smoke and sparks, hurling the weapon one hundred and fifty meters into the air before it began its terminal descent towards the hapless Chinese howitzer.

Gillette crouched on his haunches and watched the trail of smoke disappear into a veil of dark cloud, tracking the missile's flight until it re-emerged a moment later, hurtling down on the Chinese howitzer from above like the fist of a vengeful god.

The Javelin struck the PLZ-05 flush and obliterated the great self-propelled gun in a shattering fireball of flames and a cacophony of ground-shaking thunder. Bright white light seared the sky for an instant and then the world turned red with fire and fury. Pieces of steel shrapnel were flung hundreds of yards across the compound and then the broken carcass of the howitzer was engulfed in oily black smoke, and a secondary flash of explosion. The Chinese artillerymen who had been serving the gun were immolated in the fierce fireball and a dozen others were gruesomely wounded. Gillette heard the wretched victims' suffering screams and gasps of terror before a great veil of dust reared up and blanketed the battleground.

"Fuckers! Die, you bastards!" Gillette snarled a savage cry of triumph.

Because Alpha Company was back at war.

Chapter 6:

Every American rifleman opened fire.

The fusillade showed as a flickering line of fiery muzzle-flashes that lit the gloom with stabbing blades of flame.

An instant later the whip-saw of chattering noise shattered the stunned Chinese compound and sent terrified half-dressed artillerymen scrabbling in terror.

Gillette watched the first moments of the firefight from the shadows of the tree line, exulting in the chaos. Then the second Javelin team fired and a few thumping heartbeats later another of the enemy's self-propelled howitzers was obliterated in a vast fireball of smoke and flames. The explosion ripped the chassis of the PLZ-05 apart; disintegrating the steel beast in the blink of an eye. Black oily cloud roiled into the sky and a wall of searing heat washed across the compound. A Chinese crewman thirty yards away from the explosion was picked up and flung through the air like a rag doll, his clothes on fire, his chest gaping shrapnel wounds. Others, closer to the epicenter of the almighty explosion, were simply vaporized to black ash. A Chinese officer, drenched in blood and staggering like a drunkard, sagged to his knees. One of his arms had been severed. He hung his head, seemed to teeter for balance for an instant, and then fell face first into the dirt and did not move again. Another sandstorm of dust was flung into the air and the Americans lining the fringe of the woods fired into it, getting hits.

Then the men of 3rd Platoon, dug in along the eastern edge of the compound, opened fire on the camp tents, intensifying the fury.

Gillette heard the sudden swell of additional stuttering gunfire as he jinked back through the undergrowth and flung himself into the firing pit beside Tonneguzzi. The XO had his M4 carbine pressed into his shoulder, firing with the rest of the men at the flittering Chinese crewmen who swirled amongst the dust and smoke. Gillette threw up his own weapon and opened fire, sighting on an enemy soldier by one of the nearest howitzers. The man was on his stomach, half-hidden by leaping shadows, trying to scramble for shelter behind the steel tracks of the Chinese vehicle. Gillette fired and saw his bullets kick up small eruptions of dirt around the stricken Chinese soldier's face. The man crawled out of sight and Gillette cursed bitter frustration.

The clock in his head began ticking; intuitively counting down the seconds and tracking the timeline of the firefight. He figured twenty seconds had passed since the first Chinese howitzer had been struck, and maybe ten seconds since the second heavy gun had been destroyed.

Surprise seemed absolute. The Chinese troops were off balance and scattering in terror. From somewhere, beneath the layer of gunfire, he could hear an enemy siren wailing and a frantic chaos of shouts and screams. Then the two M240 machine guns at the far end of the firing line added their fury to the crescendo of roaring death.

For the first few moments of the ambush the machine guns had remained silent, waiting for their opportunity. Once 3rd Platoon had opened fire, dozens of enemy soldiers had run fleeing from their tents. The M240s suddenly had a target rich environment, and the Chinese were caught in the open.

A handful of artillerymen went down in the first furious seconds of machine gun fire. A semi-naked man wearing just a white singlet was hit by a tempest of bullets and spun in a flailing pirouette; some macabre kind of paralytic dance as bloody holes were punched through his chest and torso. He was flung backwards into the body of another man and the two of them fell together, dead in the dirt. Another man sat sobbing, crouched on his haunches with his hands covering his head, cowering and wailing incoherently like a lost child in a crowded mall as bullets tore at the air all around him. Finally, he was caught in a sweeping scythe of machine gun fire and knocked onto his back, dead.

"Keep firing!" Gillette watched the ferocious onslaught, glorying in the slaughter.

"Don't let the bastards stand! Keep hitting them!"

One of the Chinese camp tents bloomed into a fireball and the staccato of semi-automatic gunfire became punctured with the echoing crump of exploding grenades. Then the first 60mm mortars began to rain down, signaling that the heavy weapons team had joined the fight.

The first mortar rounds fell well wide of the enemy tents, landing on the beaten earth of the main compound and only kicking up dust and dirt. But after a handful of ranging shots, a cluster of rounds landed flush amongst the Chinese tents. There weren't many artillerymen left to kill, but those who had hidden in the wreckage rather than run fleeing during the first hellish moments of the fight, suffered for their choice. Mortar fragments fizzed through the air, killing and maiming indiscriminately. Tents were shredded and men screamed.

"Keep shooting!" Gillette snarled whenever the fusillade of American gunfire withered for a moment. "Kill every one of the fuckers."

The third Chinese PLZ-05 self-propelled howitzer was struck by another unleashed Javelin and the fury of the explosion seemed to stun the air. It was so unexpected and so thunderous in its violence that even Gillette gaped in astonishment. The fireball of vivid light seemed to sear his eyeballs as he gawked in wonder, appalled by the hammer-blow killing force of the missile. The howitzer seemed to disappear; dissolve before his amazed gaze like a feat of savage magic, to be replaced by a pyre of black roiling smoke and a curtain of dust.

"Jesus...!" even Marion Tonneguzzi seemed breathless. "A stockpile of ammo must have gone up with the gun."

The black boiling cloud of smoke hung like a heavy blanket over the compound and through it great chunks of jagged metal debris began to fall. Then the fourth howitzer in the line took a direct hit from a Javelin and a fresh roaring fireball lit up the dawn sky. The earth trembled and a wave of heated air swept across the compound, cremating the Chinese corpses that lay in the path of the flames, engulfing others who ran blindly into the wall of fire.

The men firing from cover on either side of Gillette reloaded their M4s and in that moment of lull the fifth of the enemy howitzers exploded. Somehow, amidst all the chaos, the heroic crew of the targeted PLZ-05 had attempted to reverse the lumbering vehicle out of its sandbagged revetment. The heavy howitzer veered blindly backwards in an attempt to get to safety, its engine bellowing and belching great clouds of exhaust. It made no difference. The Javelin missile had been launched in 'direct attack' mode. The warhead streaked across the beaten ground like a flung arrow on a trail of sparks and a feather of smoke, striking the self-propelled broadside.

In the blink of an eye, the Chinese howitzer disappeared, swallowed up by flames and smoke and a shockwave of heated wind. A tempest of steel shrapnel fragments fizzed like lethal blades through the air, cutting down a Chinese sergeant who had somehow survived the hellish hail of American gunfire and mortar blasts up until that instant. The NCO was decapitated in the violent aftermath of the missile strike. His headless body twitched on the ground for several seconds of nerveless frenzy and then lay motionless. Gillette saw a handful of other Chinese soldiers fall, some bearing ghastly wounds, others seemingly untouched, yet still flung down by the thunder of the explosion. The ground beneath the Americans shuddered and a rain of leaves was shaken from the treetops. Then a veil of dust washed over them, turning the battlefield soft with haze.

"Keep firing!" Gillette was savagely remorseless, urging his men to maintain the carnage. He reloaded his carbine and fired again into the swirling dust, aiming at the vague silhouette of a running enemy soldier who appeared suddenly through the haze. He missed, fired again, and missed again. "Don't let them stand. Don't let them get organized. Keep hitting the fuckers with everything we've got."

More deafening explosions rang out, spaced just a few seconds apart, each one a thunderclap of violence followed a heartbeat later by an echo of sound that slammed against Gillette's eardrums. The dust was struck through by flames and fresh towers of black billowing smoke.

On the eastern edge of the artillery park, where 3rd Platoon were dug in, the sound of small arms fire began to wane into a sporadic patter. Gillette sensed the lull and barked at his RTO.

"Get Third platoon on comms," he snapped. "Tell them to keep pouring on the pressure."

The RTO ducked down, turned his back to the cacophony of noise and repeated Gillette's orders over the company net.

"Three-Six says his men are running low on ammo," the RTO relayed the reply.

Gillette swore. "Fuck!"

The dust from the explosions was beginning to lift and through the shredding curtain of haze he could see that all eight Chinese howitzers had been destroyed. The most recently struck vehicles were still burning fiercely, flames leaping high into the dawning sky. The other devastated guns were nothing more than scorched black carcasses of twisted smoldering metal. The Chinese battery had been completely obliterated by the Javelins – but there were still dozens of enemy artillerymen and maintenance crewmen alive.

Suddenly a rattle of light machine gun fire echoed across the flat beaten earth and the trees above Gillette's head were peppered with a flurry of bullets.

"The Chinese are starting to fight back!" Tonneguzzi sounded incredulous. "We need to pull out."

Gillette stared for an instant and then seemed to become consumed by an unholy fury. The fact that the Chinese troops dared to defy his will both offended and outraged him. Another staccato of wild enemy fire sprayed the bushes.

Gillette glanced down at his wristwatch. It was 0352. Seven minutes had elapsed since the first Chinese howitzer had exploded. He made his decision.

"We're going to attack the fuckers!" he swore.

"What?" Tonneguzzi looked appalled.

"We're going to finish every one of those bastards off," Gillette pressed his lips into a thin bloodless line. "You stay here with Second platoon and the two M240s to cover the assault." He turned quickly to his RTO. "Get Third platoon back on comms. Tell them to attack. Attack!"

"Buck!" Tonneguzzi stopped firing his weapon and recoiled in disbelief. He seized Gillette's arm. "Why? The howitzers have been destroyed. Our mission is completed. We need to start exfiltrating back to the river."

"The job's not over until every one of those Chinese bastards are dead," Gillette felt the red mist of his rage boiling in his blood.

He seized the radio handset and ordered the mortars to stop firing and then clambered out of the hollow and stood with his back to the compound, facing the ragged line of American infantry.

"First platoon, on me, on me. Charge the fuckers!"

*

Gillette spun on his heel and burst through the undergrowth, and the men from 1st Platoon scrambled from cover and dashed after him. The troops were screaming like berserkers to suppress their natural fear. Gillette glanced over his shoulder and saw his men swarming forward. The grim set of his face turned into a ferocious smile as a surge of exhilaration ran through him.

"Kill them all!" he shrieked and fired from his hip into the dust and the smoke swirling ahead of him. "Hunt them down!"

Gunfire chattered all around him, barking and urgent. Gillette heard his heart thumping in his chest and the heavy slap of his own boots on the beaten ground. It was a hundred and fifty paces to the nearest destroyed howitzer and the closest enemy tents; a killing field – if the Chinese could organize themselves into heroic pockets of resistance.

"Don't let them stand!" his voice seemed to reach the chilling discord that verged on insanity. "Cut them to pieces!"

Behind him he heard the grunts of his men and the gasping rasp of their breath as they pounded along in his wake. Some of the troops were still screaming like fiends but others had turned grim and silent, cursing and growling without any coherent form. Their eyes were bloodshot, their faces smeared with sweat-streaked grime. They burst through the dust-storm and into an eerie ghostly world of smoke and fire and screams and blood.

A Chinese machine gun opened fire from somewhere amongst the chaos ahead of the Americans and two men went down, plucked back as if by invisible strings. Gillette saw a man out of the corner of his eye punched backwards, a scream of agony in his throat as he folded to the dirt. Then someone close behind him swore venomously and clutched at his leg, shrieking in cruel pain.

"Take out the machine guns!"

The Americans reached the nearest blazing howitzer and then finally they were amongst the chaotic maze of the Chinese tents. Some of the tents had collapsed. Two were on fire, burning fiercely. Others were just dark smoke-shrouded silhouettes, shredded by mortar fire and deep in shadow. Twisted ropes lay like slithering snakes across the ground and the contents of some tents were strewn in the narrow spaces between each row. Here and there, Gillette saw dead Chinese soldiers, their bodies flung down in attitudes of torture. Blood soaked the hard earth, staining it dark brown in great spattered patches.

He flattened himself against the canvas side of a tent, hugging the flimsy wall, keeping in the shadows, his eyes moving everywhere, his breathing quick and shallow while all around him screams and gunfire rang out. He felt his nerves screw tight and in that instant the fear came upon him; the dread of death and failure, heavy as a ton of steel, so that his knees buckled and it took every ounce of his willpower to suppress the sensation. His mouth felt dry, and his heart pounded like a drum.

He reached the corner of the tent, made a tight savage face to muster his rage, then spun around, out into the open with the M4 slung on his hip, his teeth bared, and his eyes narrowed.

Two Chinese soldiers were lying in the dirt on their stomachs, one man hunkered down behind a bipoded light machine gun, his partner close beside him feeding a belt of fresh ammunition through the weapon's breech. The gunner had his hands on the trigger of the machine gun, his teeth bared, snarling like a vengeful slaughterman as the recoil of the roaring weapon juddered up his arms.

The Chinese men were twenty yards away, firing through a narrow gap between the tents at the Americans as they surged through the smoke and into sudden view. Gillette braced his stance and fired a quick burst from the M4 carbine, punching bloody holes in both members of the machine gun team. The gunner slumped dead over his weapon and the loader rolled onto his back, screaming from bullet wounds to his hip and shoulder. He drew his knees up to his chest and clutched at his guts. Gillette fired again; two more quick roars of gunfire and the screaming stopped abruptly.

He turned to a sudden fresh spray of defiant gunshots and sighted two more Chinese soldiers thirty yards away across a patch of firelit ground. The enemy soldiers were kneeling, shooting into the smoke. He fired instinctively at the targets and missed. The two Chinese ducked down behind an overturned wooden table and were lost in the shadows.

"Shit!" Gillette cursed.

He had the sense that he had lost all control of the attack. The fighting had devolved into a hectic frenzy of flitting shadows and stabbing muzzle flashes. The screams of men dying mingled with the chatter of roaring gunfire and the curses of those who were wounded. Flames leaped high into the sky and over it all hung a heavy blanket of black smoke, smudging shapes and obscuring others so that each man seemed to be fighting on his own. There was no way he could regain order; the only choice was to continue fighting until there was no Chinese left to kill.

Two riflemen from 1st Platoon staggered out of the shadows. Their faces were tight rictuses, their features frozen into gruesome snarls. One was spattered in blood, his face masked in ghastly rivulets from a bullet graze that had creased his brow. The other man was breathless and retching, doubled over, vomit dribbling from his chin. His eyes were glassy and feverish with the horror.

Gillette motioned to the two men with a curt jerk of his hand. "There!" he pointed towards the table across the clearing. "Two Chinese fuckers, both armed. Come with me. We're going to take them out."

They moved around the rear of the tent with the intention of encircling the two Chinese. Another tent loomed out of the smoke and gloom directly ahead of them. It was larger than the other tents on the compound, the east-facing wall shredded by mortar fragments. Gillette crept close to a gape in the canvas and peeked inside. He saw a lamp hanging from an upright post diffusing a yellow glow, and a long table against one side of the interior. The table was crammed with comms gear and there were two Chinese operators, standing hunched at the radios, their bodies tight with harried tension. They were wearing headphones and relaying urgent instructions while a third man in an officer's uniform stood behind them barking orders.

Then something on a cot in the far corner caught Gillette's eye and he peered hard. Draped in dark shadows and bound to the steel frame of the bed was the limp body of a young woman. She was naked from the waist down, her corpse drenched in blood.

"Both of you hold your positions," Gillette breathed into the closest man's ear. "I will go in through the front. Once I open fire, you join the attack."

The two riflemen nodded reluctantly. One turned to cover their rear. They both felt vulnerable and exposed in the flickering firelight as the gunfire around them seemed to reach a crescendo. They shrank down into kneeling positions to make themselves less conspicuous.

Gillette crept along the length of the canvas wall, then braced himself at the tent's opening. He brought his M4 up to his shoulder, took a last ragged breath, and then charged through the hanging flaps and into the soft yellow glow of the lamp. The Chinese officer reacted first, turning his head in surprise and then instinctively snatching for the sidearm on his hip. Gillette shot the man twice from close range and then swung his carbine neatly onto the two radio operators. At the same instant the two riflemen from 1st Platoon fired through the tattered canvas wall, killing both enemy radiomen and punching holes in the bank of radio gear before Gillette could fire. Sparks flared and the expensive communications equipment disintegrated into debris.

Gillette's face was set into a savage snarl. He released the breath he had been holding and then nudged the Chinese officer's body with his boot to be sure the man was dead. He beckoned the two riflemen to follow him. "Come on. There's more killing to do."

The trio broke from the shadows and stepped into a narrow lane between two tent rows. The alley resembled a gruesome slaughter yard. Chinese bodies lay thick on the ground; dark lumpen shapes in twisted ruins. One man had been disemboweled by a burst of gunfire; another's face was so ravaged by bullets that his head was nothing more than a mangled pulp of raw flesh and shattered bone fragments. A man lay on his back with one of his eyeballs resting on his cheek and half his head stoved in. Blood and gore the color of custard dripped like slime from the tent walls and puddled on the ground.

One of the riflemen behind Gillette gagged and retched explosively. The smell of fresh blood, mixed with the putrid stench of guts and burning flesh, coated the back of Gillette's throat and made his own stomach heave.

"Come on!" he screwed up his resolve and led the two men on a scampering run towards the sounds of more gunfire.

They reached the ruins of a collapsed tent and found a small knot of fellow riflemen engaged in a firefight against a handful of stubborn Chinese. The enemy had taken cover in a shallow drainage ditch at the edge of the compound, backdropped by dense forest trees.

"The fuckers are dug in and putting up a fight!" the lieutenant leading 3rd Platoon gave Gillette a short, succinct SITREP. The lieutenant's cheek was bleeding from a cut, and his eyes were red-rimmed from smoke. "I've lost two men already and – *fuck!*" a savage spray of Chinese automatic fire made the officer clamp his hand to his helmet and duck his head urgently behind cover. The Americans were holed up behind a couple of abandoned jeep-like Chinese BJ2022 4x4 utility vehicles. Bullets whizzed and ricocheted off the steel and kicked up plumes of dust from the ground.

"How many of them?" Gillette needed to know.

The lieutenant shrugged. "Six or seven, well armed."

Gillette glanced around, looking for a solution. The sounds of gunfire and explosions, incredibly, seemed to rise in intensity; the thumping clamor underpinned by a new indistinct rumbling roar of sound that he couldn't identify.

From what he saw in the brief moment that he took to survey the battlefield, Gillette judged the firefight was almost at an end. Dead Chinese artillerymen and maintenance crew members lay scattered in great ghastly heaps, and most of the tents were ablaze or reduced to tangled ruins. One of the Chinese had fallen into a burning pyre and the stench of his roasting flesh drifted across the compound and mingled with the oily smoke from the burning howitzers. Through the haze he could see several of his men combing the ruins, checking the dead. Other riflemen were on their haunches tending to cuts and wounds. Some were stretched out on the ground and being tended to by medics. Only this handful of stoic enemy soldiers stood in the way of his total triumph.

He had lost sight of his RTO in the first few frantic moments of fighting and now Gillette searched for the man amongst the remnants of 1st Platoon. "We get the FIST on comms and order our mortars to pop smoke – and then we go in after the bastards," he decided.

The lieutenant leading 3rd Platoon looked appalled. "Sir, we could just hit them with direct mortar fire."

"They're too close," Gillette judged, dismissing the idea almost immediately. Mortars were not the most accurate battlefield weapons, and with just one hundred paces separating the two groups of combatants, the last thing Gillette needed was a tragic blue-on-blue incident from a misdirected undershot.

Then suddenly a fresh sound filled the battleground; a bellowing roar that challenged the sky and echoed like a great wounded beast through the palisade of surrounding forest.

Gillette felt a sudden chill of dreadful foreboding; a premonition of doom.

Five Chinese troop-trucks, their rear trays crammed with armed soldiers suddenly appeared at the compound gates amidst a swirling thunderhead of dust. The trucks were big six-wheelers, each carrying a full platoon of armed men. They roared into sight from behind the wall of forest trees in great belching clouds of diesel smoke, their engines revving and urgent.

"Fuck!" Gillette gasped, aghast. He felt the blood drain from his face and for a moment he peered stunned and dismayed, paralyzed with disbelief. Then an unholy rage came upon him; a murderous violence that erupted in a spitting torrent of vile abuse.

"The fucking Brit Rangers! This is their fault. Those bastards claimed they surveiled this entire sector."

"What do we do?" the 3rd Platoon lieutenant's face flushed, the urgent tone of his voice betraying his rising panic.

Gillette shoved aside his savage loathing for the British troops and forced himself to think. The five Chinese trucks were spreading out across the compound and beginning to slow. At any moment all hell was going to break loose.

Gillette snarled and then punched the steel side of the Chinese 4x4 with livid impotence. Though the ignominy of it galled him, he knew there was only one option. "Retreat," he spoke softly, and then lifted his voice so that it carried above the cracks of sporadic gunfire that still shook the air. "First and Third platoons, retreat to the woods. Move! Move! Move!"

The Americans went backwards, some running, some retreating but still in good order, facing the enemy. The wounded hobbled or were dragged, clutching at their injuries, leaving spattered trails of bright blood in their wake. The humiliation stung Gillette's eyes. He had been so close to complete and utter triumph, and now the glory of that victory had been snatched away from him – by the British Rangers who had failed to report the presence of enemy troops in the sector. He cursed bitterly beneath his breath as he joined the withdrawal, a lump of shame choking thick in his throat.

The Chinese infantry dismounted behind their trucks, using the bulk of the heavy vehicles to shelter them from erratic American fire. A whistle blew three shrill notes and an instant later the night sky was lit up by a Chinese flare, turning the dawn as bright as daylight. Two more flares went up into the air, arcing high over the compound and seeming to hang, suspended below the clouds for several seconds.

"Christ!" Gillette cursed. The Americans were cruelly exposed; easy targets for the Chinese. "Run!" he barked at his men, feeling his body cringe with the tension of dread, anticipating the sudden chatter of enemy machine guns at any moment.

The forest wall was a hundred paces ahead; a dark dense blanket of shelter but between the Americans and the safety of that gloomy veil was open ground and behind them was a vengeful enemy.

A Chinese machine gun opened fire, and another enemy flare flashed across the sullen sky.

The ground around the running Americans erupted. Two riflemen went down in the first few furious seconds, collapsing to the dirt, their legs taken from beneath them. The first rifleman was hit in the small of the back and folded forward, his arms flung outstretched, his weapon sliding from his nerveless fingers. He crashed face-first into the dirt, kicking up a cloud of dust, a shrill scream of white-hot agony in his throat and blood soaking his uniform.

The second man was struck in the thigh and crippled by the pain. His leg exploded into savage jolts of searing torture, and he clutched at the wound, blood gushing between his fingers. The corporal trailing him gripped the wounded man around the waist and dragged him towards the trees, straining from the effort while the bleeding man screamed a high-pitched keening sound in his ear.

The first Americans reached the shadowed fringe of the woods and crashed through, swallowed up by the illusory cover of darkness. Behind them the enemy infantry spread out and began to advance. The Chinese machine gun was mounted on one of the trucks with a clear field of fire, allowing the infantry on the ground to move forward unobstructed. Ahead of them they saw a running, panic-filled enemy and they were keen to close for the kill. Mario Tonneguzzi watched the enemy come on from within the dark trees and narrowed his eyes in ruthless calculation.

"Second platoon... fire!" he screamed the order, and a fusillade of flame-spitting automatic gunfire exploded from the fringe of the trees. The Chinese were caught completely by surprise and a ripple of shock washed through their ranks. Then men began falling and the compound echoed from a fresh thunder of chattering fury and the crump of explosions. A grenade thrown from the tree line fell well short of the Chinese, but kicked up a volcano of dust, veiling the retreat of the last few Americans to reach the cover of the words while all along the firing line the well-disciplined men of 2nd Platoon worked their weapons like their lives depended on it.

"Keep pouring fire on 'em!"

"Ammo! I need more ammo."

"Why aren't the fucking mortars firing?"

Gillette was one of the last retreating men to reach the cover of the forest. He ran with his arms pumping and his chest burning, his breath sawing across his throat and the heavy burden of his kit and equipment weighing on his legs. Enemy bullets plucked at the ground around his ankles and whizzed past his face, so close that he felt the heat of their passage buffet his cheek. He crashed through a high leafy bush and almost slammed into a tree. The dark of the woods enveloped him, and he flung himself down into the earthy mulch that covered the ground. He was trembling with the physical strain and the ignominy of his humiliation. His outraged loathing for the British Rangers was amplified by the deadly price he and his men had paid for poor intelligence.

He came up onto his knees, his uniform drenched in sweat and spattered in Chinese blood and peered out across the chaos of the compound.

The violence of 2nd Platoon's surprise attack had stunned the Chinese and driven them to ground. They were spread out across the compound, firing wildly into the trees. The battlefield was dark again, lit by flickering muzzle flashes. Then suddenly the Chinese were going backwards, summonsed by a flurry of short, urgent whistle blasts for no apparent reason. Gillette stared, bewildered. He knew that if the Chinese continued to advance, they would overrun the American positions. He didn't have enough men to hold off a concerted attack.

So why was the enemy suddenly falling back?

He sensed the tempo of the firefight begin to wane and the Chinese withdrew out of effective range, the sound of whistles becoming more strident.

Were they re-assembling to make a fresh assault? Were they going to ferry men forward into the firefight aboard the trucks?

He licked his lips. His mouth was dry, his throat parched. The vile odor of roasting flesh was still in his nostrils, making his stomach heave. He looked around himself and saw a handful of his men being tended to by medics and realized his troops were in no condition to fend off a second enemy assault.

He waited for a lull in the clamor of gunfire and then blundered in the dark gloom until he found Mario Tonneguzzi. The XO had his M4 pressed into his shoulder and was firing into the gloom, urging the men around him to harass the Chinese as they fell back towards their trucks. Here and there, the Chinese infantry still retorted with a frenzy of small arms fire, but they were quickly disengaging.

"Mario, we need to withdraw towards the river before the enemy can organize for another attack."

The XO blinked, then slowly lowered his weapon. The fighting frenzy faded from Tonneguzzi's eyes, and his clarity returned. He nodded, then seemed to exhale a long deep breath. "Okay."

Tonneguzzi clambered wearily from behind cover and barked at the men. "Cease firing. We're falling back."

At the exact moment the XO rose to his feet, a Chinese machine gunner squeezed off one final frustrated burst of bullets into the tree line. One round tore through the leafy undergrowth on the fringe of the forest and struck Mario Tonneguzzi flush in the throat. The XO's head snapped back and a gush of blood splashed Gillette's face. The air in Mario Tonneguzzi's lungs escaped in a great groan and he fell backwards, his eyes huge with astonishment and glassy with shock.

"Mario!" Gillette screamed.

He dropped to his knees and pulled the limp body of the XO to him. Blood was bubbling from between Tonneguzzi's fingers, and his breath rattled and gurgled in his lungs. The XO's face was pale as marble, and his gaze was unfocused. Gillette peeled off the stricken man's helmet and bellowed, his voice cracking with desperation.

"Medic! Medic!"

Tonneguzzi's fingers fluttered, and his hands shook with a palsy of tremors.

"Stay with me, Mario!" Gillette clamped his own hand over the mangled, ruined flesh of his XO's throat. Blood ran warm and sticky as treacle through his fingers. Tonneguzzi's head lolled to one side, and he began to choke. Bright red blood spilled from between his lips and dribbled down his chin.

"Medic!"

Tonneguzzi's gaze cleared for an instant and slammed into focus. Suddenly he was lucid. He locked eyes with Gillette –

and his lips formed a hideously distorted grimace of pain. Then he died with a last exhausted gasp.

For long disbelieving seconds Gillette gaped, and then slowly his face crumpled in anguish.

"Mario!" he croaked.

Gillette pulled the dead man to him and felt his chest wrench with grief; a torturous pain more excruciating than any physical wound.

Two medics arrived, their care-worn faces exhausted and haggard, but they were too late. Mario Tonneguzzi was dead.

Gillette staggered away and cried out his anguish; an incoherent bellow without form, then pressed his hands to his face as if to mask the horror. His fingers were bloody, his wrists spattered with guts and gore.

It was 0400 hours; the time his attack had been scheduled to commence.

Instead, the fight was already over.

And now Alpha Company's mournful retreat to the river with their dead and wounded was all that remained.

Chapter 7:

The retreat through the forest was cloaked in a funereal pall of gloom. Gillette trudged through the undergrowth alone at the head of the column, tortured with conflicting emotions of misery and rage. Behind him the men plodded in a long file, the wounded being helped by their comrades, the dead being carried on litters. Those who had survived the firefight unscathed walked, slumped with lethargy and indifference, their eyes haunted by the horrors they had endured and the ghastly visions that would plague their nightmares.

Gillette's uniform was stiff with dried blood, spattered with gore and reeked of sweat and fear. His chest ached and his breath wheezed in his throat. His legs felt like lead and the small cuts and grazes across his cheek and knuckles were swollen and inflamed, oozing pale lymph. But it was in his eyes where his true pain showed.

Only Lieutenant Geyer seemed immune to the sense of desolation and defeat that clouded the retreat. The craggy-faced New Yorker worked his way to the front of the column and fell into step beside Gillette.

A massive scowl concealed his concern. "Anything you need, captain?" Geyer cast a sideway glance.

"To be left alone," Gillette snapped.

"Yeah, I understand that," the FIST lieutenant said informally, "but when we get back to camp, there will need to be arrangements made, sir."

"Arrangements?"

"For the dead, sir," Geyer softened his voice respectfully.

Gillette said nothing.

The dead.

Mario. And the others; six men killed in action, and another handful wounded – some of them so badly that they might not recover. It was a cruel reminder to Gillette of the consequences of his impulsive charge into the Chinese compound. In the pursuit of glory and triumph good men had been killed.

"I'll speak to the battalion XO when we return to base," Gillette said vaguely. "I expect he will make all the necessary arrangements."

Geyer said no more and discretely fell back into the body of the column.

Two hours later, with early morning light filtering through the treetops, the column finally reached the north side of the bailey bridge. A six-man patrol were on guard. They watched the column approach from behind a wall of sandbags, silently appalled at the sight of the survivors. Gillette and his men looked like the bedraggled undead; ghostly grey-faced and haggard.

A sergeant commanding the sentry detachment made a comms report back to base, then rose from behind cover. He stared with incredulity, first at Gillette, and then at the assembly of battle-scarred men of Alpha Company who stood, dull and swaying with fatigue.

"Captain Gillette?" the sergeant was from Charlie Company and the face that stared back at him was gaunt and streaked with dust and dried blood, like a ghoul risen from the grave.

"Yes."

"Lieutenant Colonel Reilly is waiting for you, sir," the sergeant said respectfully, but tinged with a hint of foreboding. "And we have medics on standby to tend to your wounded. There is an Oshkosh parked on the far side of the bridge, waiting to take you back to base."

Gillette shook his head. "I'll stay with my men – the living and the dead. We'll walk into camp as a unit."

*

Alpha Company traipsed into camp an hour after sunrise, spattered with blood, streaked with dirt, some men limping, some dragging their feet with exhaustion, and others carried on litters, moaning pitifully in pain.

The encampment was bustling with a kind of restrained frenetic energy that perplexed Gillette. Groups of men from Bravo and Charlie Companies were attentively cleaning their weapons or squaring away their kits while beneath the dappled shade of several camouflage nets supply officers busily sorted through crates of rations, distributing them amongst the troops. The tantalizing smell of cooked chow emanating from the mess tent made Gillette's eyes water, and he realized with a sudden pang of hunger that he had not eaten in twenty-four hours.

The return of Alpha Company was greeted with a silent macabre fascination that spread through the encampment as hundreds of men turned to stare, distracted from their labor for a ghoulish moment as the battle-scarred survivors trudged past. Gillette felt cold appraising eyes on him but was too tired to give the veiled looks of the bystanders any significance.

He supervised the delivery of the wounded to the aid tent and watched those men who had the will and the energy shuffle to the mess tent. The rest of the company made for their cots, craving rest and sleep, and Gillette went with them.

He had barely stepped inside his own tent before the battalion XO, Major Guy Yee, entered unannounced, blinking in the sudden gloom. The major's kindly features seemed to convulse when he saw Gillette's blood-stained uniform and the mask of dust and spattered gore that covered his face.

"Jesus!" Major Yee gasped a shuddering reaction. "Are you wounded?"

Gillette shook his head. His senses seemed dulled so that his words came out slightly slurred. "Some of the blood is from the Chinese we killed. Some of it is Mario Tonneguzzi's blood."

Major Yee grimaced, reluctant to ask the question but knowing that he must. "Was Lieutenant Tonneguzzi wounded?"

"No, sir. He's dead," Gillette reported with bitter regret. "He was shot during the last few seconds of the firefight. It happened just as we began to exfiltrate the edge of the forest from where we had launched our attack."

"I am sorry," Major Yee's face softened with sympathy. He looked solemn as an undertaker.

Gillette said nothing, and for several long moments there was just awkward silence. Gillette felt himself sway on his feet with fatigue and he eyed his cot, craving the oblivion of sleep, but Major Yee drew a sharp breath and manfully continued. "I'm afraid rest and a hot meal will have to wait," Yee grimaced. "The Colonel is waiting for you in his tent. He wants a full mission debriefing. I'm to escort you."

"Escort me?" Gillette looked up sharply with a sudden clench of warning. "Why? What does that mean?"

"It means we get to share a delightful stroll together in the morning sun," Major Yee tried an avuncular smile, and then swift distraction. "But you need to change, shave, shower and shit first. You look like hell."

*

Gillette followed Major Yee across the crowded base towards the Battalion TOC (Tactical Operations Center). As the men walked, the major turned several times and smiled over his shoulder at Gillette, as if to offer kindly reassurance, until Gillette felt himself tense with a creeping premonition of suspicion. Finally, Gillette stopped stubbornly in the middle of the compound amongst a crowd of other soldiers, forcing the major to backtrack.

"What's going on?" Gillette frowned.

"Going on?" the major asked blithely, as if not understanding the question. "I told you. The Colonel wants an immediate mission debriefing."

"Then why have you been sent to escort me?"

Major Yee's friendly smile turned watery. He made a tortured face and then tried to shrug the question off. "Protocol," he lied.

Gillette's own features drew tight. "Am I under some kind of investigation? Is this a briefing or an interrogation?"

Major Yee looked appalled by the suggestion. "Of course not, man!" he blustered.

"Then what's going on?" Gillette put an edge into his voice that made several of the bystanders suddenly stop their work and look towards the two officers with curiosity.

Major Yee looked suddenly flustered. His face suffused with color that might have been cringing discomfiture. The major was not Gillette's idea of a fighting man. In fact, Gillette had often wondered how Yee had ever risen through the ranks. He pictured a younger version of the officer facing him and tried to imagine Yee up to his elbows in blood and gore, fighting in a trench – and failed. Yee had been a career soldier in the years when the world was largely a peaceful place. Perhaps he had served overseas, maybe in Japan or Australia; far away from combat hot spots. Perhaps he had been transferred from some administration post into a combat unit at the outbreak of war. He did not have the tough exterior of a veteran fighting man, or the confident swagger of a soldier who had proved himself under enemy fire. Yee would have made a good politician, Gillette conceded – but a warrior, leading others into the fiery crucible of death and danger?

No.

Yee was a good man, a kindly officer, and probably a good administrator. Not for the first time, Gillette pictured the major as a country pastor, benevolently tending to a flock of elderly churchgoers.

The brief exchange had attracted a small crowd of idle spectators. Yee, aware that they were drawing unwanted attention, leaned close to Gillette and whispered.

"You took too much upon yourself. You went beyond your orders – again. The Colonel is rightly furious. He wants answers."

So, it would be an interrogation.

Gillette narrowed his eyes and belligerently thrust out his jaw, oblivious to the crowd that watched on. "I did what had to be done," he snapped in defiant defense of his actions. "I seized the advantage in a combat situation and executed my orders to the best of my ability under the circumstances."

*

Two Oshkosh M-ATVs were parked outside the battalion TOC, one vehicle with its engine still running. The M1087 EVAN (Expandable Van Shelter) was sited close to Colonel Reilly's own tent and connected to a running generator. Ladders on either side of the truck led up to doorways into the heart of the Op Center. The interior was crowded with electronics, desks, telephones, maps, laptops and a handful of staff all crammed close together.

"Wait here," Major Yee ordered Gillette, then clambered up the steps alone and paused inside the open doorway. After a moment the major came back down the steps and pointed.

"The Colonel is waiting for us in his tent. Follow me."

There was an armed sentry waiting outside Colonel Reilly's tent. Yee stepped past the guard with Gillette at his shoulder. The interior was cool and smelled of cigar smoke and sweat.

Lieutenant Colonel Reilly was seated behind his desk, his head down over a sheaf of papers and his brow creased by a frown. He shook his head slowly, scratched a note in the margin of a page, then laid the paperwork down and raised cold intimidating eyes to glare fixedly at Gillette.

Gillette felt a shiver of apprehension under the steel of the Colonel's menacing gaze. The mood inside the tent turned hostile and frosty.

"Did you fully understand the orders I gave you for the attack on the Chinese howitzers, Captain Gillette?"

"Yes, sir," Gillette answered, and then decided he could best defend himself by being completely honest. "Except for the involvement of the platoon of British Rangers," he confessed. "I made a mistake, sir. I had assumed those men were part of the mission and would be involved in the fighting, until I was abruptly informed by their lieutenant at the attack site that they were not, in fact, going to join the battle."

"Lieutenant Loftus."

"Sir?"

"That was the British officer's name. Lieutenant Loftus."

Gillette frowned. Reilly seemed to be missing the point entirely and Gillette saw an opportunity.

"Well, sir, Lieutenant Loftus informed me that the British were not going to join the battle. They left, sir. They simply abandoned my company and disappeared back into the forest. Presumably they returned here to camp for a mug of hot tea while my men did all the killing," he added derisively.

"And that was your only mistake? Your only misunderstanding?" Reilly glowered; his eyes blazing.

"Yes, sir," Gillette fixed his gaze on the far wall of the tent, staring at a dark stain an inch above the Lieutenant Colonel's head. "I admit my error, sir. Once I realized my company would be the only ones fighting the enemy, I sent Third platoon around to the eastern side of the compound, to take up the ambush positions I had initially planned for the Brits to occupy."

Reilly nodded. He looked haggard, the flesh of his face ashen and sagging in folds beneath his eyes and along his jawline. "The rest of your orders were clear?"

"Yes, sir. Perfectly clear."

Reilly suddenly threw down the pen he was holding, then bounded out of his chair and paced behind his desk, too irate to remain seated. The Lieutenant Colonel looked like a lion, prowling the confines of a cage. The interior of the tent fell ominously silent, broken only by the hum of the TOC's generator and the revving of an Oshkosh's engine.

"If you clearly understood your orders, then why did you launch your Javelin attack on the enemy howitzers at 0345?" Reilly stopped and snapped suddenly. "Your orders were clear and precise. You were to launch your Javelin assault on the Chinese artillery exactly at 0400 hours."

Gillette flinched and flushed with awkwardness. Reilly smiled menacingly. "I know all the details of your attack, Captain Gillette," he said with oily warning. "I have a full report on my desk. The timeline of events was relayed to me by a four-man British SAS team, codenamed Bravo Three-One. They've been operating in the forests north of the Yalu River on long-range surveillance missions for the past six weeks. They were the unit who first located the Chinese battery. They called in their British Ranger counterparts to surveil the site. You never saw them, but Bravo Three-One maintained observation throughout your mission."

Gillette blinked. His first instinctive reaction was outrage. "Sir!" he growled. "I resent my company being spied on!"

"Your attack was under observation by the British," Reilly's voice rose, shouting down Gillette's protest, "because this was a British operation, Captain Gillette."

Gillette flinched. Reilly's spiteful retort had taken him by surprise, as had the revelation that the Brits were the ones who had planned and orchestrated the operation. "But I thought –"

Reilly cut Gillette off, the senior officer's voice rising further. "I know damned well what you thought. You thought this entire attack was all about you, and your ego. You thought you and your men were the centerpiece of this whole operation because your damned conceit cannot conceive of anything more important than yourself," Reilly spat pure venom, and his face turned mottled with patches of red rage. "Now, answer the damned question, Captain," the Lieutenant Colonel emphasized the word 'captain' as if it implied a veiled warning. "Why did you launch your first Javelin fifteen full minutes before your ordered time to attack the Chinese howitzers?"

"Sir," Gillette felt himself reeling like a boxer struck consecutive stunning blows. He felt off-balance and disoriented. "When we reached the attack point along the southern fringe of the enemy compound and the British Rangers moved off, abandoning me, I observed with Lieutenant Tonneguzzi that the Chinese artillery crews suddenly ceased firing. I watched for several minutes, then realized that the enemy were changing crew teams, or perhaps pausing to re-supply their heavy guns with fresh munitions. The compound became dark without the howitzers firing and at that moment I realized I could seize a tactical advantage."

"What advantage?" Reilly came from around his desk and stood toe-to-toe with Gillette. The Lieutenant Colonel stood three inches shorter but seemed to bristle with pent-up aggression.

"The element of surprise, mixed with the cover of darkness," Gillette said, and as the words spilled from his mouth, he realized how lame the explanation sounded.

"You already had the element of surprise," Reilly pointed out acidly. "And there was no need for the cover of darkness, captain. Not for a firefight from the shelter of the forest. The only reason to utilize the cover of darkness would be if you had a premeditated intention of storming the compound in an infantry assault."

"Yes, sir," Gillette was utterly exposed.

Reilly looked appalled. He withered Gillette with a look of sick contempt. "So, you had planned to charge the enemy artillerymen right from the outset, despite your clear orders to remain in the trees and to ignore the Chinese gun crews?"

"Sir, it wasn't like that," Gillette blustered. "The sudden darkness across the Chinese compound presented a new set of circumstances that hadn't been factored into my orders. I am a warrior. I saw an unexpected opportunity to destroy the Chinese howitzers and annihilate over a hundred important enemy troops."

"So, you acted on your own initiative – yet again."

"I acted as any good soldier would in the prevailing combat circumstances," Gillette said stiffly.

Reilly rounded on Gillette, like a bull who has sighted the matador's red cape. "Don't you dare compare yourself to a good soldier, Captain Gillette," the Colonel hissed, visibly trembling to restrain himself. "You're nothing of the type. You're the worst leader in this battalion; the most egotistical, arrogant and conceited officer I've ever had the misfortune to command."

Gillette felt like he had been slapped hard across the face and he railed against the tirade of abuse. "My record is exemplary, sir!"

"That's the problem, Gillette. You. Your record. Your triumphs, your glory-hunting thirst for attention and the spotlight. You think you're the only man in this army that matters. You think you're smarter than your senior officers. You think you're some kind of superhero soldier. Well, you're not," Colonel Reilly unleashed his savage appraisal. "You get men killed chasing plaudits. You're not heroic – you're an ego-driven glory hunter."

"Sir," Gillette felt his fists bunch and his body strain to the edge of physical violence. "I resent your comments."

"I don't give a shit how you feel, captain. We're way past army rulebook and regulation protocol right now. How many men were killed during your reckless charge across the Chinese compound and the firefight that followed?"

"Six, sir," Gillette clenched his jaw and spat the words. "And a handful of others were wounded."

"Six," Reilly said. "Six men killed unnecessarily because you wanted to storm the enemy compound and make yourself out as a military hero, despite clear orders to remain in the woods and fire from good cover."

Gillette said nothing. His eyes glowed red with rage. Standing in the corner, veiled in shadow, Major Yee watched on in excruciating discomfort.

"And Lieutenant Tonneguzzi," Reilly reminded Gillette.

"Yes, sir."

"And thirty-two British Rangers. You killed them too."

"What?" Gillette's head snapped up, his face twisted with outrage and his eyes monstrous with shock. He looked at Colonel Reilly, appalled at the suggestion. "That is a lie!" he defended himself. "The damned Brit REMF cowards retreated before the fight even began."

Reilly suddenly looked dreadful with grief and in an instant the crackling tension in the room turned chilling and sinister.

"I told you this was a British operation," Reilly began, his voice now hollow. "Your attack against the Chinese howitzers was nothing but a diversion, Captain Gillette. You think this war is all about you, like you're the star of a Hollywood film, but it's not. Your mission was to attack the Chinese artillery park and draw the enemy's reserves away from a secret Chinese communications node that the SAS discovered over a month ago."

"What?" Gillette gaped.

"The enemy comms node was four clicks away from the artillery park, hidden in an underground bunker," Reilly went on, each new word like a fist to Gillette's churning guts. "The site was protected by a motorized company of Chinese troops concealed in a camouflaged hangar. Your attack was designed merely to lure that protection detail away from the communications node so the platoon of British Rangers could launch an attack."

"Sir," Gillette stammered. "I... I didn't know..." his voice croaked.

"Those men you called 'damned Brit REMF cowards' knew they were most likely going to their deaths, but they went anyhow, Captain," Reilly bludgeoned Gillette mercilessly, his voice chilling as ice. "Your early assault left them stranded two miles away from their objective at zero hour, but they still rushed forward and attacked regardless. Your immediate retreat once the enemy reserves had been lured away gave the Chinese security detail time to re-mount their trucks and return to the communications bunker before the British could complete their assault. All thirty-two Rangers, including Lieutenant Loftus were slaughtered."

Gillette said nothing but the rigidity left his body, and his face seemed to crumple. He felt a weight crush down on his shoulders so that his knees went soft beneath him, and he swayed.

"You had one job, Captain Gillette; attack the Chinese howitzers as a diversion and then remain in the woods and open fire," Colonel Reilly hissed. "If you had followed those orders, the Chinese security patrol defending the communications node would have responded to the raised alarm and been delayed by the ensuing firefight with your men, allowing the British Rangers to successfully mount their assault on a vital enemy site. But, because you attacked early, and because you charged the compound, you were forced to quickly retreat when the enemy's reserve detail arrived. As you were falling back through the forest, carrying your dead and wounded, those enemy soldiers returned to the comms node and wiped out the Rangers. You might as well have put a gun to the heads of the British soldiers and executed every one of those brave heroic men yourself."

Gillette felt his throat constrict and his breath jam in his chest; a white-hot pain of horror that choked him. His eyes turned dread-filled as the brutal consequences of his impulsive actions were revealed.

"As a result, the entire battalion has now been ordered forward," the Colonel went on grimly. "Our orders are to mount a full-scale attack on the Chinese communications node before the enemy can rush in reinforcements from the outskirts of Dandong." Colonel Reilly gave a heavy sigh and then returned to his desk. He sat down, pensive and burdened by foreboding. "I wonder, Captain Gillette," he looked up grimly one last time, "how many more men will die today as a consequence of your glory-hunting failure to obey orders?"

*

The long trudge back across the compound was like a walk of shame for Gillette. He sensed the malevolent, pitiless eyes of others watching him and the burden of his guilt turned his legs leaden. Nothing remained a secret for long in a military camp, and he was sure that already whispered word of his catastrophic dawn action and the consequences of his decisions were already spreading like wildfire within the ranks of the battalion.

He walked on in horrid and embarrassed silence, his head held high, but his guts twisted in pangs of burning humiliation. At his side walked 'Daddy' Yee, keeping pace and staring stony-faced off into the distance. When Gillette reached his tent, he ducked inside, grateful for the solace, desperate to be left alone with his misery.

Gillette dropped down onto his cot, numb and shattered. His career was in tatters. And he was hurt. He had led his men through fire and fury and gore and blood. He had always been at the forefront of every battle, leading by example. He had believed the fearless heroics of his actions and the daring way he had commanded his troops would attract the admiring attention of his superiors who would value his audacious action-man attitude.

Now he realized, rather than being admired, he was despised – and in a moment of painful self-analysis, he understood the derision was deserved. He had taken too many risks with other men's lives. He had elevated himself and his own personal glory-seeking aspirations above good soldiering.

He felt crushed, and ashamed.

And guilt-ridden.

He had loathed the British Rangers; derided them as cowardly REMFs. Now he realized just how fiercely heroic those quiet unassuming men had been. They had gone to their deaths, betrayed by his own actions, and yet still they had charged against impossible odds and without protest.

Gillette felt unworthy of them and the sacrifice they had made.

He buried his face in his hands and felt tears prickle and sting his eyes. He hadn't wept since he was a child. Major Yee, acutely uncomfortable, looked away until Gillette composed himself.

"You have one chance to redeem yourself, Razor," the major spoke softly, gentling his words. "Colonel Reilly wants to relieve you of command – and he may well do so – but not right now. There's no time because the battalion is moving out in two hours to launch our attack on the Chinese comms node. And with Lieutenant Tonneguzzi dead, there is no immediate and apparent replacement to lead Alpha Company. So, you have a chance – a final chance to make things right."

Gillette looked up slowly. Major Yee was standing over the cot, his face filled with a mixture of human compassion and professional contempt.

Outside it began to rain.

Gillette nodded, understanding. He wished he was alone with his desolation and self-pity.

"There will be a briefing in the Colonel's tent in one hour," Major Yee went on.

Gillette balked. The notion of facing his fellow company commanders and their leadership groups made him cringe.

The rain began to fall harder, spattering on the roof of the small tent as a squall swept across the compound. Major Yee tried to force his features into an encouraging smile but failed. "Get your shit together. The battalion still needs you. We've got a mission to finish, and you've got a job to do. You owe it as a debt of honor to the British Rangers and the men from Alpha Company who died today."

*

By the time Gillette returned to Colonel Reilly's tent an hour later, the interior had been transformed. The paper-strewn desk was still in place, but the rest of the interior had been filled with wooden easels upon which had been displayed a series of grainy intelligence photographs.

Gillette sidled cautiously into the tent, like a cat entering a strange room, wary and on edge. The small space was crowded with the battalion's other officers and the air was stuffy. Gillette felt accusing eyes on him, but he kept his expression stony. Colonel Reilly acknowledged him with a curt nod. Major Yee eased his way through the press of sweaty bodies, grim-faced and downcast, until he stood at Gillette's side in a shadowed corner.

"It's going to be a bitch," the major opined in a whisper. "The enemy comms node is like a damned medieval stronghold. Stone, steel and concrete," he shook his head.

Gillette peered past the major and studied the grainy photographs on the easels more carefully. Three were high-altitude spy satellite images and two were taken from ground level, probably through a telephoto lens, judging by the quality.

The satellite photos were stamped with altitude, latitude and longitude references. They were black and white pictures that showed a small, lightly wooded section of anonymous forest, with an obscure, vaguely rectangle shape in the center of each photo which had been circled in red. But even though the location of the Chinese bunker had been identified in each image, Gillette still struggled to recognize a clear man-made shape.

The two ground-level photographs were only slightly more revealing. They were amateur-looking color shots of large sliding steel doors, joined in the middle, and streaked with green and brown paint. The photographs had been taken from two locations, showing slightly different angles.

The other officers in the room stood studying the images with the same intent scrutiny as Gillette, muttering in quiet, serious voices amongst themselves. Colonel Reilly stood in front of his desk and called for silence. All heads in the tent turned.

"Gentlemen, in an hour from now we are marching into harm's way," the Colonel began gravely. "Our objective is to destroy a critical Chinese communications node located in a forest five clicks to the north of here," he paused for a moment to let the gravity of his words sink in. "This is an important mission. Command believes this enemy comms bunker is part of a vital communications network through which the Chinese are marshaling their forces for the defense of Dandong city. Take out the bunker and we severely inhibit the enemy's ability to coordinate their attacks; take out this bunker, and the fight for Dandong might be won in days instead of months," Reilly said.

The silence from the assembled battalion officers was absolute. Colonel Reilly reached for a fistful of papers on his desk and began reciting snippets of information.

"The site was located by British SAS operatives several weeks ago and it has been under surveillance by British Rangers ever since. We understand the bunker is underground and that the only apparent entry point are the two steel doors you can see in the ground photos. Those images were taken by an SAS patrol who will meet us north of the Yalu River and guide us to our attack point."

The mention of the Rangers and the SAS made Gillette wince and flush red. He wondered if the British team were the same men who had observed his inglorious pre-dawn attack on the Chinese artillery park.

"This is not going to be a covert mission," Colonel Reilly went on. "At dawn this morning a surprise attack on the bunker by our British Ranger friends who had planned to break open the doors with HE charges was thwarted by a company of Chinese infantry who deployed to defend the installation. Those Chinese troops are based here, in a camouflaged hangar," he strode across the tent to one of the satellite images and stabbed at a non-descript clump of forest about a mile from the target. "The enemy will now be on high alert and anticipating another attack. No doubt the Chinese will be rushing troops east from Dandong, and perhaps sending men from bases further north to fend off our assault. Our best hope of success is to launch our strike before any reinforcements can arrive."

Gillette let out a small strained breath of relief he had been holding. Reilly's description of the failed Ranger assault had adroitly left him and his reckless actions unmentioned, and he felt a twinge of gratitude. Reilly could have castigated him in front of his fellow officers and made his ignominious humiliation complete. That the Colonel had chosen not to do so was a measure of the man's admirable integrity.

"With stealth no longer a factor, the USAF has agreed to place two F15EX Eagles on standby in the air space southeast of the river, armed with GBU-72 bunker busters," Colonel Reilly went on, staring into the faces of the officers around him but never once making eye contact with Gillette directly. "Once the battalion is in position and ready to mount our attack, a JTAC (Joint Terminal Attack Controller) will call on those fighter jets to launch their missiles at the target. Our job will be to go in after the explosions and destroy what is left of the enemy, and their equipment. Do you all understand?"

"Yes, sir!" the assembled officers chorused.

"Bravo Company will play defense," Reilly singled out the unit's captain and got eye-to-eye with the man. "Your boys will take up positions to the west of the site and defend the dirt road that connects the enemy troop hangar to the communications node. The instant we attack, the Chinese reinforcements will rush to defend the bunker. It's your task to hold that force off until the assault on the comms node is successful."

"Yes, sir."

"Charlie Company will lead the attack on the bunker," Reilly searched the room for Charlie Company's leadership group. He caught sight of the captain and his XO standing beside one of the easels. The captain was a young, competent officer with a lean face and intense eyes. "You will go in after the bunker busters. We expect the comms node to be a myriad of underground tunnel-connected rooms. Kill everyone. Destroy all the equipment."

"Yes, sir."

"Alpha Company will remain in reserve and will not fight unless needed," Reilly looked down at the notes in his hand, a deliberate distraction to avoid glancing at Gillette, then looked up again, the briefing complete. "That is all. Inform your men, and get your gear sorted. We move out at 1300 hours."

Chapter 8:

The battalion formed into loose ranks and marched north from the compound under leaden grey skies and wind-driven curtains of rain. The dense Chinese forest beyond the Yalu made vehicular movement impossible, so the Oshkosh M-ATVs and transport trucks were left behind, compelling the men to lug their heavy equipment on their backs.

Once beyond the bailey bridge, Bravo Company took the lead and a platoon of men were detailed to point duty, moving ahead of the battalion in skirmish order. The footworn path north turned into a slippery mud-soaked quagmire, and progress slowed.

Colonel Reilly stepped to the side of the trail and checked his watch fretfully. Alpha Company under Gillette's command marched at the rear of the unwieldy column. The troops were surly and downcast, their faces tight with simmering resentment. They were good men who had been poorly led, and without the mollifying influence of Lieutenant Tonneguzzi to placate them, they were brooding with discontent for their captain.

Gillette was aware of his men's bitter mood yet felt powerless to reassert his authority. He trudged on alone and isolated, his eyes on the ground, feeling shrunken with indignation.

An hour into the arduous march, two shabby unkempt men suddenly materialized from the woods beside the trail. They appeared like ghosts, emerging silently from the trees. They were both small-framed men, bearded and bedraggled. Their hair was greasy on their shoulders and their faces were black with grime. Their uniforms were indistinguishable, but their weapons were meticulously well maintained.

"SAS," one of the strangers introduced himself laconically to a startled Bravo company soldier who had been scouting ahead of the main column. "Where is Reilly?" The stranger had a broad English accent.

The British operatives were escorted back down the line. Colonel Reilly met them both by the side of the walking trail.

"22 SAS. I'm Lang. This is McReedy," one of the British soldiers said simply. "We're here to lead your men to the attack point, Colonel."

Reilly nodded, dumbstruck. The two SAS soldiers looked like wild mountain men. They had been surviving covertly in hostile enemy territory for weeks on end without showering or shaving.

"Very well," the Colonel gruffed.

With the two SAS soldiers leading the way, Reilly felt unburdened of some responsibility, and he turned his fret-filled thoughts to the impending attack on the Chinese installation, questioning his plan, wrestling with alternatives and contingencies. The rain intensified. The heavy swollen clouds overhead sank lower to the ground, so they appeared to brush the treetops. The light turned gloomy, and the air trembled with rumbling thunder.

The march north seemed unending, even to Gillette and the men from Alpha Company, who had trudged much of this same torturous trail the night before. Finally, the column veered off the narrow earthen path and the men began working their way further eastwards, navigating a clumsy passage through thick woods, undergrowth and muddy sloping ground.

By the time the column shuffled to a halt, it was the middle of the afternoon and the men were heaving with exhaustion.

The two tireless SAS operatives led Colonel Reilly and his company commanders forward, creeping like thieves through the forest. The ground underfoot was muddy and the air ripe with the scent of decaying wet vegetation. The rain softened to a grey mist that mingled with the men's sweat, so their sodden uniforms clung to their bodies like a clammy second skin. Gillette went forward with the others, his instincts on high alert, his guts tripping with uncertainty. The ground around them rose gradually and progress became a slippery slog. They reached the crest of a gentle rise, slithering forward in the mud on their stomachs.

"There's the enemy target," one of the SAS whispered, then pointed away into the distance.

From the crest of the elevated rise, Reilly and his company captains peered north across a thousand yards of sparsely wooded shallow valley – and saw nothing for several moments until gradually the edges of an angular shape began to emerge in the distance. It was like a mirage, Gillette realized; something so vague in appearance that if he looked away, he was sure he would not find it again. The straight lines of a low wall began to emerge, blurred by the misting rain and masterful camouflage so that he had to force his tormented mind to full focus to hold the shape in sight.

The longer Gillette peered, the more apparent the shape in the distance began. Through a filter of trees, he saw the outline of a low parallel roof, and then a section of wall with a rise of grassy ground against it. He realized that, like an iceberg, he was staring at just the upper tip of the bunker. Most probably there would be air ducts and ventilation grills camouflaged on the rooftop and perhaps high-powered electronics antennae obscured from view by the tangle of surrounding trees. Even parts of the rooftop seemed overgrown with clumps of bush and grass to fracture the unnatural geometric construction lines.

After several minutes, the SAS men moved back off the crest and continued further to the east with Reilly and his battalion leadership group trailing. When the SAS operatives finally paused again, they were behind a low buttress of slick grey rocks. One of the men pointed.

Reilly and his officers cautiously lifted their heads above the cover of the rocks and Gillette saw it immediately this time; the horizontal line of the bunker's camouflaged roof and two square doors, almost facing him directly. Although they were nearly a mile away from the target, he didn't need his binoculars to recognize the paint-camouflaged steel doors from the grainy photographs he had been shown at the Colonel's briefing.

"That's the entrance," one of the SAS men muttered.

Colonel Reilly and Charlie company's captain got their heads close together and studied the gently sloping terrain through binoculars. The captain grunted. The ground appeared relatively even, covered in patches of knee-high grass and ragged rocky outcrops, indispersed with clumps of small trees and thorny bushes. Colonel Reilly grunted.

"It looks too neat," he muttered darkly.

"It looks like a trap," Charlie Company's captain agreed.

"It might be mined."

"It's not," one of the SAS cut across the conversation. "We've completed a night recce of the ground to within a hundred yards of the bunker," the Special Air Service operative said. "Best guess is the Chinese cleared the area when they built the installation and what you're looking at is regrowth. There are no mines."

The man's word was good enough for Colonel Reilly. The British SAS were widely regarded as the most accomplished and well-trained soldiers anywhere in the world.

"Fine," he nodded and set aside his concerns, then instead began to study the terrain, picturing the attack going in.

"The enemy know their installation has been compromised," the Charlie Company captain frowned, speaking his private fears aloud. "They might have set up machine gun posts in the far tree line, anticipating another attack."

"We'll have to take that chance," Colonel Reilly said. "Once the bunker buster strikes the target, you will lead your men in," he decided. "Get amongst the debris of the tunnels and kill everyone you find. Destroy all the equipment. Leave nothing, understand?"

The captain nodded, and Reilly, his decision made, turned back to the SAS operator. "What about the Chinese troops detailed to protect the facility? Where are they located?"

The SAS man pulled a grubby creased map from a pocket and laid it out on the ground behind the wall of rocks. The map was damp and dirt stained.

"Here," he pressed his finger at the map, pointing to an area to the north west of their position.

"And the dirt road?"

"Here," the operator drew a line with his fingertip because the road was not shown on the map.

"We need to intercept their trucks," Reilly looked first to the map and then into the eyes of the SAS man. "Recommendations?"

The operator did not hesitate. He knew the terrain like the back of his hand. "Set your men up on the verge of the trail," he said. "Once the bunker is hit, the Chinese troops will be immediately dispatched. If you can mount a successful ambush, you can hold them up."

"One Chinese company?" Reilly wanted confirmation.

"Three now," the SAS man shook his head and delivered the news Reilly had been dreading. "Seven more troop trucks arrived at midday, but no heavy equipment has arrived yet. But my best guess is that it will be on its way. I figure you'll be up against three hundred enemy infantry, give or take a few."

"Damn," the Colonel grimaced. He glanced skyward. Rainclouds were sweeping in over the treetops, pushed along by a nagging chill wind. The heavy overcast turned the afternoon dark and menacing and the rain drummed for a relentless minute then eased up into a grey curtain of showery haze.

"Lead the way."

Reilly left Charlie Company's captain and his leadership group to plan their attack on the bunker, then ordered Gillette's men from Alpha Company to remain with Major Yee and the battalion's HQ element while he and the troops from Bravo Company followed the two SAS on a circuitous trek through more forest.

The men headed west, backtracking, first to rejoin the trail that had brought them north from the compound, and then continuing further westward towards the destroyed Chinese artillery park. After two arduous miles of blundering through a dense maze of more trees, the SAS operators began to veer north.

Reilly kept his eyes on the cloud-filled sky seen through the canopy of forest foliage as the march towards the dirt trail became a test of endurance. The SAS were tireless, moving like specters ahead of the column until the two operatives finally paused, then dropped stealthily to their haunches. Reilly waved the column of marching men to a halt and went forward with Bravo Company's captain and XO.

From a hundred yards away, and through a veil of trees, he saw a stretch of brown gravel road, running from his left to right.

"Show me," Reilly wanted to inspect the dirt trail.

They went on, taking minimal precautions until they reached the road.

"The bunker is about a click to the east of here," one of the SAS men stood in the middle of the dirt track and pointed away to his right. "This trail runs for another five hundred yards then peters out. This is the only route to the comms node."

Reilly nodded. He and Bravo Company's captain walked a length of the track together until they had a sense of the landscape. The dirt path was just wide enough for a single lane of trucks and was fringed on both sides by thick clumps of scrub. It seemed a perfect site for an ambush. The far side of the road was lightly wooded ground for several hundred yards before the forest wall thickened.

They crept back to the waiting column before either man dared speak.

"I don't like the position, sir," Bravo Company's captain made the startling declaration.

Colonel Reilly looked the man a sharp silent question, inviting him to explain.

"If we site our Javelins to target the enemy trucks when they first appear, we'll block the road."

"Exactly," Reilly nodded. That was the point. It would stall the Chinese column and prevent them from reaching the comms node.

"But once the road is blocked, the Chinese will spill out into the surrounding forest, sir," Bravo Company's captain went on. "They might be able to outflank us."

"Your option?" Reilly's face tightened but he pressed himself to patience.

"Forget the Javelins, sir. Let the convoy draw past us and then hit the first and last truck with small arms fire and grenades. The fight will be at close range and the enemy will be confused."

Reilly shook his head. "No." He didn't want a close-combat engagement with a numerically superior enemy if he could avoid it. The notion of holding the Chinese at arm's length was much more appealing. It would be easier to disengage from the fighting if the battle went against the Americans.

"But, sir..." the young captain tried again. Reilly cut him off with a brusque shake of his head.

"Get your men into place, captain," Reilly ordered, the matter decided. "Do it quickly and quietly. We have to expect Chinese patrols. The enemy are anticipating an attack. They will be on high alert. I want no sound; nothing that might draw attention until every man is in place along the verge of the road."

Reilly beckoned an RTO with a wave of his hand and got on comms to Major Yee back at HQ.

"Bravo Company is moving up into ambush positions. We are a mile to your north west. I am staying here to command the attack. In exactly twenty minutes from now, I want you to order the JTAC to call in the Eagles."

*

For the tenth time, Major Guy Yee checked his watch and sighed with rising anxiety. He flicked a sideways glance at Gillette. The two men were standing close together with the battalion's headquarters element three hundred yards to the rear of Charlie Company's positions.

The men of Alpha Company were dispersed discretely amidst the forest trees, resting and talking quietly. Smoking was forbidden so the men sat miserable and lumpen with their brooding discontent while the rain continued to fall.

Major Yee checked his watch again and made the face of an undertaker.

"It's time."

He strode to the JTAC and told the operator to whistle up the waiting Eagles. "Give them the go order," the major intoned gravely, "for an immediate strike."

When he returned to Gillette's side, the major's face was rumpled with creases of concern. "All we can do now," Major Yee said sagely, "is tuck our heads between our knees and kiss our asses goodbye. Everything is in the hands of the gods."

"I'm going forward to watch," Gillette said and looked into the fraught major's face, either as a challenge or a provocation. Major Yee nodded, then reluctantly followed in dutiful resignation.

They reached the ring of low rocky elevated ground where Charlie Company were positioned, the men tensed, and tight-faced, waiting to attack.

For several long seconds the two officers stood still and listening with vague expectation. The rain pattered from the treetops and a man somewhere behind them coughed and hawked up a glob of phlegm. The forest was very still, the silence seeming to press in around them from every side.

Then suddenly the unmistakable sound of fighter jet engines echoed against the clouds, many miles away but coming closer with every passing second. The roar seemed to fill the sky but had no clear direction, reverberating across the heavens.

Gillette knew the fighters would approach from the east so he turned in that direction expectantly, but through the forest canopy he could see nothing but grey thunderheads. He felt himself draw tense, and his heart began to race with a squirt of adrenalin.

The two F-15EX Eagle II 'Super Eagles' were the latest generation of Eagle fighter jets that had originally begun operations back in the 1970s. The F-15EX's were the last word in fourth-generation multirole combat jets and had only recently been rushed into service following the outbreak of war. They were fast, fitted with cutting-edge technology and sensor systems, and able to carry a massive payload of ordnance into action.

By the verge of the dirt road and surrounded by the men of Bravo Company who had taken up their ambush positions, Colonel Reilly heard the sounds of the approaching fighters and looked up. He saw them for just a few seconds; dark insect-like shapes in the distance, suspended high in the sky and stark against a white bank of boiling cloud. The two Eagles were in sight just long enough for the lead fighter jet to release its deadly payload – and then they were gone again, climbing steeply into the heavens.

The GBU-72 Advanced 5K Penetrator was a five-thousand-pound class precision guided bomb equipped with tailfins to steer its route to target. The sophisticated targeting suite in the F-15EX released the weapon on course and the JDAM GPS-based INS (Inertial Navigation System) on board the guided bomb unit activated to provide in-flight guidance. The weapon had been developed to take out hardened and deeply-buried enemy targets and had been designed to punch through heavily reinforced structures before exploding.

Reilly saw the GBU-72 drop from the F-15, and he tried to follow the bomb's plummeting flight towards the Chinese bunker. The munition appeared as a blurred streak as it fell earthwards, then was lost against the backdrop of a dark thunderhead to be replaced by an unnerving whistle as the heavy weapon made its terminal descent.

Reilly stood, waiting and watching apprehensively – and then the sky over his shoulder seemed to erupt into a mighty fireball of flame and smoke.

The GBU struck the Chinese comms bunker with a direct hit, penetrating deep through the ground and the concrete walls of the installation before detonating. The explosion was cataclysmically ear-shattering, and then the force of the shockwave swept through the surrounding forest, uprooting small trees and bending others almost double. A great curtain of choking dust and dirt blew through the woods like a sandstorm and Reilly, despite standing a thousand yards away from the impact point of the massive explosion and protected by a dense palisade of forest, had the good sense to fling himself to the ground just in time.

The shockwave swept past, dragging behind it a curtain of dust and small debris, but still the echo of the explosion seemed to continue. The ground shook and the fireball climbed high into the sky, boiling amidst a rising tower of black choking smoke.

"Jesus wept…" Bravo Company's captain watched the monstrous pall of billowing flames through the veil of forest trees with a sense of shock and profound awe.

Gillette, Major Yee and the men of Charlie Company witnessed the GBU-72 strike from behind a shallow fold in the ground and sheltered by a palisade of rocky outcrops. But even though they were hundreds of yards away from the impact point and in cover, the force of the shockwave knocked men off their feet and tore through the treetops, bringing down a hailstorm of leaves and branches. Gillette felt the ground beneath him shudder and heave, and then the violent roar of the explosion cracked against his ears.

He closed his eyes and felt a hot rush of howling wind sear his face and then a flail of dust and dirt pummeled him. Too late, he ducked down for better cover, his ears ringing and bright white light burning inside his eyelids.

When he opened his eyes again and peered cautiously over the top of a boulder, he saw a monstrous fireball climbing high into the sky and a swirling column of smoke. Pieces of rubble, chunks of shattered concrete and clumps of gouged dirt began to fall from the sky, raining down like volcanic debris. A fragment of jagged concrete went whistling through the forest, smashing off branches overhead, shot out from the epicenter of the explosion like a mortar shell.

"Christ!" one of the men crouched beside Gillette gasped and then clamped his hand to his helmet and tucked himself into a ball on the ground. "Fuck! Fuck! Fuck!" the man's panic rose to a wail as small stones and pieces of twisted metal blew like shrapnel through the forest.

A piece of concrete cracked against the rock Gillette was hunkered down behind and shattered into splinters of dust. A branch nearby snapped and fell crashing to the ground, narrowly missing two men. The curtain of dust kicked up by the surging eruption was a thick swirling soup of brown haze that fell like powder, and the rumble of the explosion went on and on like a violent assault against the ears.

In the numbed, shocking silence that followed the explosion, Gillette rose slowly to his feet, covered in ash and dirt, like a man emerging from the aftermath of a freeway car crash. His ears were ringing, and he felt unsteady on his feet. He swayed like a drunkard and blinked through the swirling dust storm. For several seconds he could see nothing. Then, slowly, the billowing filth seemed to thin and mingle with the great plumes of black smoke rising from the clearing.

The GBU had left a vast crater in the ground, heaving up the earth in every direction so that ground zero looked like the rim of a volcano. The sparse scatter of trees around the explosion site had been flattened, and patches of nearby grass were on fire. Twisted chunks of concrete and iron – some the size of cars – had been flung upwards and outwards by the savage force of the blast and lay strewn across the valley floor while from within the great gaping hole smoke and flames still poured.

Gillette gaped in astonished awe. "Fuck...!" he croaked with chilled wonder.

Major Yee, clutching one hand to a bleeding cut on his cheek, stumbled forward and looked on with the same macabre fascination. The major's face was grey with ash and dust, his jaw hanging slack. "Surely no one could survive that," he rasped.

The stunned silence drew out. The smoke climbed higher into the sky and mingled with the black swollen thunderheads. The leaping flames cast an eerie red glow over the belly of the clouds.

Then, a single voice rose from out of the awed hush; a voice filled with raw determination and resolve.

"Charlie Company on me!" the captain leading the assault on the bunker cried out. "Go! Go! Go! Attack!"

*

Gillette watched the troops of Charlie Company emerge from their cover and go swarming down the gentle slope of the rise, down into the valley towards the devastation of the Chinese bunker. He felt a twist of jealous envy tighten in his guts and wished he were part of the attack. He heard the sergeants barking at their men and he saw the line of attackers spread out, still running forward in a crouch, scrabbling over the loose ground and past fallen trees.

Beside Gillette, Major Yee watched Charlie Company's advance through his binoculars. He found the company captain at the forefront of the attack and kept the man framed in the glasses. The captain was gesticulating to his men, waving his arms to spread them out, urging them to keep advancing, and Yee felt himself tense with dreadful foreboding. The company was still six hundred yards from the site of the explosion and if any Chinese soldiers had somehow survived the cataclysmic bomb blast – or if the Chinese had anticipated a frontal assault and had set up machine gun nests in the far trees – this was the moment they would open fire; when the American infantry were vulnerable and exposed in plain sight and without cover.

The major clenched his jaw and felt a knot of anxiety choke in his throat. He turned to the west and the high-powered lenses slid past a wall of magnified trees until he was peering towards Bravo Company's positions. A clock in his head began ticking. He figured two minutes had passed since the GBU had detonated. If the Chinese security detachment were on high alert, they would be already clambering into their trucks and speeding towards the site.

Of Bravo Company or the dirt road, Yee could see nothing through the dense forest, but he knew that if the fighting kicked off, the sounds of combat would carry clearly.

Momentarily relieved by the tense silence that persisted, he turned his binoculars back to Charlie Company and heard himself muttering earnest encouragement.

"That's it!" he cheered in a tight whisper. "Keep going. Keep pushing ahead. Don't stop, dammit. Faster! Faster!"

Gillette found himself infected by the battalion XO's anxiety, bristling like a dog on the leash to join the attack. He searched the distant tree line, looking for any sign of Chinese troops waiting in ambush but saw nothing but a vast expanse of debris blanketed by black smoke.

"They're going to make it," he heard himself, his voice hoarse. "It's going to be okay. If the Chinese were waiting for us, they would have opened fire by now."

Charlie company began to move more cautiously as they closed on the crater. The open ground gave way to clumps of concrete and steel that provided cover and the men began to falter, proceeding in small groups like they were advancing along a rubble-strewn city street.

Still the sinister fraught silence persisted, adding to the tension.

"Keep moving!" Charlie Company's captain frantically gestured to his troops, running from cover to cover, bent double to make himself a smaller target. "Follow me!"

Then suddenly the men were amongst the upheaved earth and heavy concrete slabs, on the very lip of the crater. Black boiling smoke washed over them. Twisted steel beams of melted metal blocked their way and although the fireball of the explosion had long burned itself out, still the heat from the mouth of the crater was searing as the open door of a great furnace.

The captain stood for a moment and peered down into the void of horror the GBU had created. It was a scene of devastation he had never seen the likes of before. The crater was many meters deep and the banks of the vast hole were black and ragged. Below him he could see sections of broken concrete slab and more twisted metal. Smoke was venting from the craggy aperture, pouring up into the sky as if through a chimney. The smoke was lit by fires that were still burning from somewhere deep within the ground.

"Come on!" the captain croaked and turned to seek out his platoon leaders. "Let's get in there like hogs and root the bastards out!"

Gillette and Major Yee both relaxed with gusting sighs of relief. The threat of a surprise enemy attack was over. Now the assault on the Chinese bunker would be a tunnel fight; a grim, dour close-quarters clean-up as the men went through each space searching for survivors and destroying enemy comms equipment. The risk of an ambush and slaughter had passed: the battle was not over but triumph now seemed assured.

Yee turned and blushed a smile at Gillette. The major felt slightly foolish. He had feared disaster, and it had not eventuated. He let out the breath he had been holding and lowered his binoculars. "That went better than I had hoped for," the kindly major confessed. "I was worried."

And then another explosion erupted; a deep rumble of violent noise that cracked and echoed through the trees, sounding from the west where Bravo Company were lying in wait; a bleak reminder to the major that the mission was not yet a success.

Because the real fight was just about to begin.

Chapter 9:

Colonel Reilly checked his watch with a sense of rising anxiety.

One minute had elapsed since the explosion. He imagined the scene around the bomb site; visualized the dust and debris still falling from the sky as Charlie Company went down into the valley floor towards the fireball, their weapons ready as they closed on the Chinese comms bunker. Then, with an effort, he jerked his attention back to the task at hand.

"Steady."

He looked along the ambush line. Bravo Company were concealed in the fringe of undergrowth that bordered the dirt road, ten yards inside the tree line. The men were hidden in shallow scrapes of ground or behind fallen logs. They were fretting and overwrought in the still silence, weapons locked and loaded.

He checked his watch again.

Ninety seconds.

"Stay calm. Remember to make every shot count."

The Javelin teams were positioned at the western end of the line, covering a bend in the road from where they would be first to sight the approaching Chinese trucks. The M240s were at the eastern end of the ambush line where the dirt road petered out. Between those two points were scattered the rest of the company, including the command element with the company's captain and his XO both crawling between clusters of men to offer final words of bantered bravado or earnest instruction.

Two minutes.

The sound of the approaching Chinese convoy was muted by the hiss of persistent rain through the tree tops so that for a moment, even though he was alert and anticipating it, Colonel Reilly remained unaware of the impending danger until he sensed men around him begin to tense. He cocked his ear in an attitude of absolute concentration and after another fraught moment heard the oncoming sound, rumbling and revving through the distant forest.

He felt his body clench tight with strain.

"Wait until you have clear targets to fire at!"

The sound of the approaching Chinese troop trucks grew steadily louder, their belching diesel engines straining with urgency as the drivers crunched up through the gears. A man lying in the dirt close to Reilly suddenly doubled over and vomited quietly in the long grass, then wiped his mouth with the back of his hand and re-took his position in the firing line. Somewhere someone coughed, but the sound was drowned out by the enemy trucks.

Then suddenly the Chinese troop transports burst from behind a thick wall of forest and appeared at the far end of the gravel track, still perhaps a thousand yards away from the bend but coming on fast. Reilly tried to estimate the number of vehicles but through the misting rain it was impossible. They were traveling in convoy along the road, coming directly towards the waiting ambush at high speed, mud spraying up from their chunky tires, jouncing over potholes and splashing through puddles.

One of the Javelin teams fired a missile in 'direct attack' mode and the CLU kicked back like a mule against the operator's shoulder as the projectile arrowed away towards its target on a thin blue feather of smoke.

Reilly saw the launch and held his breath. A pounding heartbeat later the truck at the head of the Chinese convoy suddenly exploded, ripped apart by the hammer blow impact of the Javelin. The front of the truck disintegrated into a fireball of scorching flames and a thousand jagged shards of shrapnel went whizzing through the forest like flung daggers. Black oily smoke threw a choking blanket across the dirt trail, blinding the Americans and obscuring the rest of the convoy.

"Hold your fire!" Reilly had to raise his voice over the echo of the explosion.

The relative silence in the aftermath of the blast was unnerving. But it was not a true silence for it was punctuated by the screams of dying men and the urgent sounds of others shouting in panic. The surviving Chinese trucks slewed to a frantic halt and the infantry crammed into the rear trays spilled down off their vehicles.

Reilly cursed bitterly under his breath. He had hoped to take out two or maybe three of the enemy trucks with Javelin attacks to give his outnumbered men a fighting chance against the shocked enemy remnants. Now he had forsaken the element of surprise – but the cost to the Chinese had been minimal.

The road was blocked. The destroyed truck burned like a pyre, the metalwork blackening and then melting in the fierce heat. Some of the undergrowth beside the trail caught ablaze and began to burn through scrubland, despite the rain. Smoke towered high into the sky and crawled in thick tendrils like mist between the trees, dragging a grey veil of haze across the battlefield.

"Damn," Reilly grunted, and scratched anxiously at the unshaven stubble on his chin.

A battle plan – no matter how intricate – only lasted until the first shot had been fired. Colonel Reilly had rolled the dice, and the result had been unfavorable. Now the enemy were alert and were spilling into the surrounding forest. He had frittered away his one chance of catching the Chinese off balance.

The three companies of Chinese soldiers were not elite – but they were well trained and equipped with enough firepower to overwhelm Reilly's position. The American troops were well disciplined, and their weapons were technologically superior, but the Colonel knew those small advantages would count for little in the claustrophobic confines of a close-quarters fight across a forest floor. Reilly sensed a restless wave of unease wash through the men on either side of him. He snatched for the frequency-hopping secure Harris 148 hand-held radio that he carried and raised his voice over the chaos of frantic radio transmissions clogging the battalion net.

"Six-Six, Bravo-Six. We hold our ground," Reilly spoke to Bravo Company's captain with grim resolve. "Our mission remains the same. We fend off the Chinese until Charlie

Company have had time to clear out the enemy comms node and destroy everything. Then we fall back. Acknowledge."

Bravo Company's captain listened to his orders over the radio, his face tight with apprehension.

"Bravo-Six, Six-Six, acknowledged," the captain muttered bleakly, interpreting the Colonel's orders as, *'We're fucked. Pray for a miracle.'*

The tense silence across the forest drew out, jangling anxious men's nerves and putting them on edge. A gentle breeze through the trees rustled leaves and branches, filling the American's fields of fire with the illusion of sudden movement so that the tension ramped up almost unbearably.

"Steady!" Reilly raised his voice and snapped at the men, aware that his words would carry towards the enemy.

The smoke from the burning truck climbed higher into the air and then began to smear into the clouds. The haze drifting through the forest thinned for a moment and a sudden burst of Chinese shouts brought Reilly's head snapping around. He peered hard into the palisade of trees in front of him but could see nothing. Then the distinct coughing echo of mortar fire filtered through the trees.

The first Chinese smoke rounds landed two hundred yards beyond the Americans, blanketing their route back towards the Yalu with a wall of white-grey swirling clouds. The next smoke rounds straddled the dirt trail, landing directly amongst the American positions, creating a wave of confusion and chaos amongst Bravo Company.

The Chinese attacked.

A hundred running men broket from the green dappled wall of forest; a swarm of darting shadowed shapes, yelling like berserkers to bolster their own courage, firing wildly from the hip. They charged without cohesion, forced to clump together or break apart by the dense undergrowth. Reilly saw the enemy emerge from the distant wall of trees and drew a shocked, startled breath. The troop truck had been destroyed a thousand yards back down the road, but the Chinese had used the few confused moments since the explosion to creep forward through the undergrowth so that when they suddenly sprang to their feet, firing, they were already within a few hundred yards of the American position.

"Open fire!" he shouted, his voice rasping with shock and alarm.

The American line erupted in a spontaneous clamor of violent fire-spitting fury as the men from Bravo Company unleashed a frantic fusillade into the drifting veil of smoke that swirled and billowed across the road. For a thunderous moment the Chinese were sitting ducks, picked out against the forest and pounded by a hail of bullets. Then the smoke boiled thick and billowing amongst the American positions, cutting visibility to just a few feet and obscuring the looming menace so that their fire went wild and the Chinese closed in.

"Pick your targets!" Reilly shouted.

The sound of the charging Chinese through the undergrowth was like a wall of noise and then suddenly they were breaking through the thin shroud of smoke and bursting across the narrow gravel trail, just thirty paces from where the Americans were waiting.

"Fire!" Reilly spat.

The Chinese materialized like ghosts, running fearlessly onto the guns. The Americans cut them down in a fierce, frantic firefight. All along the line the barking chatter of automatic fire erupted as suddenly Bravo Company were overwhelmed with targets.

A Chinese sergeant and a man flanking him on either side were all cut down in a swathe of roaring fire from one of the M240s. The sergeant fell dead on the road but the men running with him staggered on, their bodies ripped apart by gaping wounds, their faces tortured and terrifying as their momentum seemed to propel them forward even though their bodies were broken. One reached the far side of the road and dropped, drenched in blood. The other teetered in the middle of the trail, his features suddenly blank with dismay until a final bullet caught him flush in the face and snapped his head backwards.

He seemed to hang, suspended for an instant in a pink mist, before falling dead to the ground.

Two more Chinese broke through the smoke, firing wildly. They were short, squat figures, running doubled-over. They launched themselves towards the verge of the road, fearlessly courageous, but were cut down by one of the four men who comprised the Colonel's PSD (Personal Security Detail). The soldier had reacted with cat-like reflexes before Reilly had time to even recognize the proximity of the threat.

The closest Chinese soldier fell in a puddle of mud, writhing in pain from a gaping wound to his chest. The man at his heels was struck in the shoulder and spun round by the impact. Blood sheeting his arm, his weapon lost, he ran on. His legs turned to rubber, and he took three more staggering steps before the riflemen fired again, hitting the enemy soldier in the throat and knocking him down.

"Keep firing!" Colonel Reilly stared at the corpse of the dead enemy soldier and felt his face flush with shock. "Hold them. Hold your ground!"

A Chinese grenade fell through the haze of smoke and exploded on the shoulder of the road, short of the American positions but still close enough to throw up a wicked storm of fragments that sliced through the undergrowth and struck a soldier in the thigh. The man grimaced in pain and rolled out of the firing line clutching at his wound with his hands and sobbing.

"Medic! For fuck's sake, I need a medic!"

More Chinese grenades exploded, tearing the tree line apart and wreaking havoc amongst Bravo Company. Two men firing from a shallow scrape of ground were flung cartwheeling into the air, their bodies broken and their uniforms shredded by shrapnel, the destruction so grievous that the corpses were barely recognizable as human. Blood splashed through the trees and ran dripping from the leaves.

The swirling smoke turned the battlefield into a chaos of confusion and fractured the fighting into small isolated bloody pockets of violence where each man in the American firing line seemed to be fighting on his own, cut off from his comrades. Reilly had no sense of whether the line was holding; all he could see were darting grey shapes in the haze, flitting in and out of sight, screaming like banshees as they charged towards the American positions.

"Hold your ground! Hold your ground!" he repeated the cry over and over again, hoping his words would carry above the roar of rifle and machine gun fire and the deep 'crump' of exploding grenades. A bullet whizzed past his face and another socked meatily into the trunk of a tree just a few feet away to his right. The soldier fighting next to the Colonel impulsively rose to his feet and fired at a clump of vague shapes in the distance, then was thrown back, knocked over by a Chinese bullet. The man fell flat in the grass, his eyes wide, his expression astonished as a trickle of bright red blood welled up between his lips and ran down his chin. Reilly stared, aghast for a moment of raw shock. The Colonel's security detail closed around him, bristling and alert as Presidential bodyguards. It was their job to protect the Colonel, and, if necessary, extract him if there was a danger of the position being overrun, or a chance the Colonel might be captured by the enemy. They threw up their weapons and returned fire at the Chinese.

In the center of the American line, the company captain and his XO were trying to maintain order as the wave of enemy soldiers reached the far side of the road. The Chinese paused there, hidden behind smoke and gathering themselves for a final charge, and Bravo Company's captain knew that he could not allow the enemy to rest or organize themselves.

"Grenades!" he shouted, then rose to a crouch and hurled a grenade into the smoke. The grenade landed in a clump of bushes and exploded. A flash of fiery light flared through the wall of grey smoke and a man in the distance screamed in agony.

"Grenades!"

Every infantry squad was equipped with M320 grenade launchers, and the Americans worked their weapons with a desperate will. Within a few thumping heartbeats the sound of the battlefield became a series of crumping explosions. Some of the launched grenades flew long and exploded harmlessly. Others lobbed amongst the milling Chinese and caused catastrophic wounds.

An enemy soldier burst through the smoke and reached the center of the trail before he was cut down by a roar of fire from the XO. Two more Chinese charged, flushed from cover by the spatter of American hand grenades that began falling along the edge of the road. The two charging men reached the far side of the track and were mercilessly cut down from close range.

Then, finally, the smoke began to thin, and the veil gradually lifted from the battlefield. Ghostly shapes became more distinct and the thin shroud of cover that had allowed the Chinese to close with near impunity began to rise, leaving the enemy vulnerable and exposed. Suddenly those grey specters became stark silhouettes, backlit against the forest foliage, and the men from Bravo Company began to take a terrible toll.

The Chinese lining the far side of the road were cruelly exposed, and too close to the American positions to withstand the concentrated hail of fire that poured into them. The sound of the firefight through the forest rose to a fury – and then the Chinese began to retreat.

They fell back, slowly at first under a hail of withering vengeful fire, their own guns still spitting defiance, until another storm of American grenades fell out of the sky and exploded in amongst them. It was the moment that turned withdrawal into retreat. The Chinese sprang to their feet and ran, and the Americans sped them to their deaths. Three fleeing Chinese were cut down by the M240 machine guns who were positioned at the far end of the line and finally had enfiladed targets in their sights. A Chinese officer, red-faced with humiliation and still screaming defiantly at his men to go forward was shot in the back as he turned away, disgraced by his men's cowardice. The spray of M4 fire caught the Chinese captain between his shoulder blades and knocked him off his feet. A sergeant, crouched cowering close to the captain, saw his officer fall and took the opportunity to bolt for his life. He threw down his weapon and ran, jinking and weaving through scrubland and between trees like a startled jackrabbit, hunted by the American guns until a well-aimed burst of M4 fire took out his running legs and threw him, screaming in sudden agony, face-down into the long grass.

"Cease fire!" Colonel Reilly cupped his hands to his mouth and bellowed the order above the firestorm of noise. "Cease fire! Cease fire!"

The abrupt silence in the aftermath of so much deafening horror was appalling. An eerie, haunted stillness crept over the forest, punctuated by shrill screams of agony. An American rifleman clamped a trembling hand over a shoulder wound, then groaned pitifully. Another soldier, further along the line, kissed a silver cross slung from a chain around his neck and then began to weep tears of relief. Bravo Company's captain rose to his haunches and cast his eyes across the scatter of men around him. Some were hunched and gasping. Others were red-eyed and ashen-faced with shock. A handful of men had minor flesh wounds. Three were dead and others were moaning in pain.

A medic who was crouched over the body of a corporal sat back on his haunches, his shoulders hunched in defeat and exhaustion. His hands were bloodied up to his elbows and his face etched with deep lines of anguish. He turned and made eye contact with the captain, then slowly shook his head.

Colonel Reilly rose cautiously from cover and peered across the stretch of dirt trail towards the distant wall of dense forest. Between that palisade of trees and where he stood were the remains of a Chinese infantry company; the scattered corpses of close to eighty men. It was a nightmarish tableau of blood and gore and devastation. Some of the dead lay in the grass in restful attitudes of sleep. Others were broken bundles of shredded blood-soaked rags, their arms flung wide, their tortured faces etched with the agony of their last few seconds. Some of the bodies were already swarming with flies. A Chinese soldier lying in the middle of the road, the purple swollen bulge of his entrails splattered across the dirt, gave a last aggrieved groan and then died. Another wounded man rose from the grass on the far side of the road and took a handful of tottering drunken steps towards the far trees before he collapsed again.

"If they launch another assault..." Bravo Company's captain appeared at the Colonel's shoulder, "I don't know if we will be able to hold them, sir." The man's drawn haggard face was spattered in blood and smeared with grime.

Colonel Reilly grunted. The Chinese had to attack again. It was inevitable.

He made his decision just as the enemy mortars began clearing their throats again and more swirling plumes of thick white smoke started to fall amongst the trees all around them; a grim prelude of what would soon follow.

The Colonel turned urgently to his RTO.

"Get Battalion HQ on the line, pronto. Tell Major Yee that I want Alpha Company brought forward to reinforce our position."

*

Major Yee acknowledged the Colonel's orders and turned quickly to Gillette. Both men were standing amongst the rocks overlooking the valley floor where Charlie Company were going about their grim work amongst the debris of the Chinese communications bunker. Gillette had been observing the operation with professional appreciation but was being kept keenly distracted by the distant rumbling thunder of firefighting that flared to the west where Bravo Company were in action.

He watched plumes of white smoke rise through the treetops of the forest canopy and heard the percussive thump of grenade explosions, gripped with a warrior's envy.

But the very last thing he expected was to be called into action, given the catastrophic consequences of his pre-dawn attack on the enemy's artillery park.

"You're up," Major Yee handed the radio receiver back to his RTO and said abruptly. "The Colonel wants Alpha

Company to reinforce Bravo Company's position immediately. They're under heavy enemy attack and in danger of being overwhelmed."

"Christ!" Gillette breathed.

He turned and sprinted back to where Alpha Company were resting behind the frontlines. The men were slouched and lazing, some sound asleep, others smoking or talking quietly amongst themselves. Gillette sensed the undercurrent of their simmering hostility as he burst into the tree-covered clearing.

"On your feet!" he barked the order. "We're moving out and heading into harm's way."

None of the men moved. They glared at him with baleful eyes, and for a sickening, stomach-tripping instant, Gillette feared the prospect of mutiny. "Bravo Company are under heavy attack. Colonel Reilly has ordered us into the fight to reinforce them."

That news seemed to break the spell of brooding resentment. This wasn't another of Gillette's glory-hunting maverick actions; it was a rescue mission. The troops all had buddies and friends in Bravo Company. The battalion was a close-knit community. The men scrambled to their feet and snatched for their equipment; their faces suddenly filled with grim purpose.

Gillette kept his features bleak and impassive, his expression never altering, but behind his steely eyes he gasped a silent breath of relief. "Move out!"

They ran.

They dashed through the forest lugging their heavy weapons and burdened by kit, their gear clunking and jangling, wrestling with their fears and apprehension, compelled by resolve and duty.

Alpha Company was on the move and charging into harm's way.

Buck Gillette was running towards a chance of redemption.

*

Chinese mortars bombarded the verge of the dirt road with smoke rounds for two relentless minutes, turning the forest floor into a grey-misted dreamscape of swirling clouds to conceal the sinister nightmare of their next advance.

Colonel Reilly peered into the dense void with a sense of cringing foreboding, his ears attuned to the slightest sounds, his senses on full alert. He could smell the sweat of the men close around him and he could hear their labored breathing. A rifleman reached for a fresh magazine for his M4 and ejected the empty mag all in the same fluid motion. He slapped the fresh thirty-round magazine into the slot, then released the bolt, stripping the top round off the new mag and seating it into the chamber. The sound of the action seemed like the crash and slam of a car door in the fraught, brittle silence.

Then there was another sound, vague and ethereal at first; a sound like a gentle rustling breeze through the treetops. Colonel Reilly frowned, and his features tightened. He peered hard into the wall of swirling smoke, trying to locate the direction of the noise but it seemed to be coming from everywhere. Then, in an instant of chill terrified understanding, he recognized the danger.

"Get ready!" he bellowed the warning. "Here they come!"

It was the sound of men's legs, brushing through long grass, drawing inexorably closer, getting louder until it seemed to surround him.

"Hold your positions!"

The smoke hung close to the ground like a winter morning's fog, writhing and twisting amongst the trees, billowing and then drifting, thickening and then briefly thinning. Dull wraithlike shapes began to emerge through the greyness, vague and indistinct, seeming to drift across the ground – too many for the Colonel to count.

"Open fire!"

Bravo Company poured a tempest of furious gunfire into the smoke and the sudden roar of noise unleashed the Chinese to their attack. The enemy began roaring their berserker-like war cries as they surged forward. They burst through the veil of smoke and came sweeping across the road as a wall of frenzied bodies.

"Fire! Fire!" Bravo Company's captain in the center of the American line took up the Colonel's urgent cry. "Hit the bastards hard!"

The smoke turned the battlefield into a pandemonium of screams, shouts and confusion, punched through with spitting muzzle-flashes of bright lurid flame. A rifleman from 1st Platoon emptied his magazine into the wall of smoke and then was set upon by a Chinese soldier who ghosted out of the haze, firing from the hip. The enemy soldier reached the far side of the road and shot the rifleman flush in the face. The dead man fell backwards into the grass and the Chinese soldier roared savage triumph before he was cut down by a vengeful burst of M4 fire from somewhere further along the American line.

A Chinese officer reached the middle of the road and turned to wave his men forward, his face alight with exultation, his voice high-pitched and urgent. Dark grey shapes ghosted past him and then an American bullet struck him in the shoulder, spinning him round like a top. He clutched at his bleeding arm, still shouting encouragement to his soldiers until a second M4 round struck him in the chest and threw him down dead in the gravel.

The Chinese washed across the dirt track like a ghostly wave; a tide of grey vague shapes moving in the swirling mist and the Americans were on the brink of being overwhelmed. Their firepower and their defensive positions were best suited to a stand-off battle, not a close-combat struggle with an enemy near enough to smell their fetid breath and the stench of their fear.

Colonel Reilly sensed the American line was beginning to waver. His men were being suffocated by the claustrophobia of the conditions. He turned and desperately searched the trees behind his position, and for a moment was tempted to call the retreat. The route back towards the bridge over the Yalu was still open. But for how much longer? If the Chinese reached the American side of the road in numbers and the firefight became a melee, his last chance to disengage would be snatched from him.

The men on either side of him were still firing, but beginning to edge nervously backwards, trying to keep the Chinese at arm's length. The smoke was still thick as soup across the ground obscuring targets and adding to the chaos. The Colonel's security detail, anticipating an imminent Chinese breakthrough, began to manhandle the Colonel away from the fighting.

An enemy soldier suddenly materialized from the void, just fifteen feet away. His face was wild, his mouth was open, and there was a maniacal scream in his throat. He saw Colonel Reilly and charged towards him. One of the Colonel's detail pushed Reilly aside and opened fire, his legs braced, his M4 slung from his hip. The weapon roared and the range was so close that the muzzle-flash seemed to leap from the barrel of the weapon and touch the running enemy soldier. The fusillade of bullets tore the Chinese soldier's body in ragged halves and left his guts spattered across the dirt.

Reilly got slowly to his feet, dazed and stunned. He gaped at the offal-like remains of blood and steaming gore and felt his gorge rise, burning like acid in the back of his throat.

Then suddenly Gillette was at the Colonel's side, broad-shouldered, his intensely-set face looming out of the smoke.

"Alpha Company reporting. Your orders, sir?"

Reilly flinched, and then his senses slammed back into focus. He seized Gillette's arm with a fierce grip. "Reinforce the right side of the line! We've got to drive the Chinese back."

Chapter 10:

Alpha Company's timely arrival saved the American position a moment before it seemed certain to collapse. Gillette's men were ferocious. They swept forward and took the battle to the Chinese, brawling and snarling like gutter fighters. Gillette was at the forefront of the counter-attack, consumed by a savage frenzy. If he bellowed orders, he did not realize it. If he swore or screamed, he did not know it. He just fought with a ruthless madness.

All around him the roar of combat rose; a melding of screams and barking guns, swelling through the smoke. A wild-eyed Chinese soldier loomed out of the haze with his uniform spattered in blood and his weapon held in his hands like a club. Gillette turned and fired reflexively, and the enemy soldier dropped out of sight, swallowed up again by the haze. Another Chinese soldier, wearing the uniform of a junior officer, materialized out of the grey fog holding a sidearm. He snatched a shot at Gillette that missed by inches, and then his eyes went wide with terror as Gillette fired back, striking the officer in the stomach and bowling him over. The man fell flat on his back, his legs thrashing, his hands clutching at his bleeding guts. Gillette fired again and the officer went very still.

"Alpha Company on me!" Gillette's voice was hoarse. "On me!"

He went forward again, the gravel of the trail under his scuffing feet, the breath in his throat burning. The air seemed heated, as if he stood at the edge of a great fire, and the noise was chaotic, punched through with the shrill screams of men dying.

"Push the bastards back! Don't let them stand!"

He fired again at a knot of grey shapes ahead of him. The enemy soldiers were running obliquely across his front, wading out of the long grass and moving away to his left. They were screaming as they charged; ghost-like shapes with malevolent intent. Gillette fired into the mass of bodies from a range of fifteen paces and the Chinese seemed to dissolve in the sights of his M4. Three men went down like they had been bowled over by an almighty fist, punched off their feet in violent splatters of blood and gore. A fourth man was struck in the hip and hobbled cruelly. He staggered on for a few more steps and then fell twitching into a clump of bushes, screaming in pain. Gillette went forward and shot the bleeding man in the chest. The three others were all dead, their bullet-riddled corpses heaped carelessly on top of each other like a petulant child's discarded dolls.

"Look out!" Gillette pointed at a Chinese soldier flitting in and out of the smoke away to his right. "Kill the fucker!"

A man from 2nd Platoon who was fighting at his captain's shoulder turned and fired.

The firefight was lurching towards its denouement. The Chinese attack had dashed itself against the break wall of the American position and begun to lose its impetus. Chinese soldiers started to drift back towards the forest wall, using the last tendrils of the drifting smoke to conceal their withdrawal. Some ran. Some dragged wounded comrades with them. A few fought on doggedly, edging backwards into the long grass but still firing in defiance. The Americans continued to shoot into the smoke until there were no more targets and only the dead remained, strewn across the blood-drenched road.

Colonel Reilly, his uniform soaked in sweat and spattered with a Chinese soldier's blood, was standing by the side of the trail in urgent conversation with Bravo Company's captain.

"That was close," Lieutenant Geyer, his rugged face bloodied from a gash above his brow, loomed out of the smoke and stood by Gillette's shoulder. He spat into the dirt, then wedged the stub of a chewed cigar into a corner of his mouth. "I thought we were fucked."

"So did I," Gillette confessed, breathing hard. He glanced left and right through the thinning smoke to check for threats but saw none. The Chinese had melted back into the forest. He let his M4 drop to his side. "Hold your fire!" he shouted the order, though it was unnecessary.

Colonel Reilly threaded his way through a scatter of dead bodies and stopped suddenly when he was level with Gillette.

"Good work," he conceded grudgingly. "Pass on my thanks to your men, then tell them to take cover on the right of our line. The Chinese will come again, and we'll need to be determined to resist them." He might have said more but an RTO suddenly dashed forward, radio handset in his fist.

"Six-Five on comms, sir."

Reilly snatched for the handset. "Six-Five, Six-Six actual," he acknowledged.

"Six-Six, Six-Five," Major Guy Yee's voice crackled and echoed through a buzz of static. "Charlie Company are touchdown! Repeat Charlie Company are touchdown. Mission complete. We are beginning to exfil towards the Yalu."

"Roger, Six-Five," Reilly felt a sudden surge of blessed relief swell up within him. The Chinese comms bunker had been destroyed. The operation was a success. "Halt your withdrawal at the northern side of the bridge until we rendezvous. Bravo and Alpha companies will begin our exfiltration immediately. Acknowledge."

"Six-Five acknowledges," Yee signed off.

The fighting was over...

Almost.

*

"The Chinese will be massing for another attack," Colonel Reilly fixed Gillette with his gaze, his tone intense in the sudden fraught aftermath of the firefight. "They don't yet realize their comms bunker has been destroyed. They're going to come at us with everything they have, and if we withdraw, they'll pursue us." Reilly paused significantly for a long moment. "So, I need a platoon of your men to hold our position while the rest of the battalion exfiltrates safely back to the banks of the Yalu."

Gillette nodded.

"Leave First platoon with me, sir," Gillette said. "We'll hold them off until you're clear of the area."

Reilly nodded, then tried to soften the implications of his order. "I only need you to buy us ten minutes."

Gillette said nothing because there was nothing left to say.

It was a suicide mission.

*

The haggard survivors of Bravo Company and the rest of Alpha Company used the last tendrils of writhing smoke screen to disguise their withdrawal, moving slowly, hampered by the burden of their wounded. They went with stealthy quiet, melting back into the dense forest. Colonel Reilly stayed behind with a handful of men.

"I'll withdraw with the rear-guard," he told Gillette quietly, the two men standing just within the cover of the trees from where they could overlook the blood soaked, corpse-littered dirt road. "Remember; hold for ten minutes and then get the hell out of here," the Colonel went on. "We're rendezvousing with Charlie Company on the north bank of the bridge. Good luck."

Gillette nodded. He had been left with around thirty men and one M240 machine gun. He stood for a long moment, peering towards the far wall of forest, searching for any sign that the Chinese were massing for their next attack. He saw nothing.

He knew thirty men could never hold off a concerted enemy assault, and he knew that ten minutes in a firefight was like a lifetime.

And he knew what all that inevitably meant.

One of the men broke across his dark brooding thoughts to ask him where to site the machine gun but Gillette did not reply immediately. Instead, he stood staring past the man, peering at the back of a broad-shouldered figure who was deepening a scrape of ground with a shovel.

"What the fuck are you doing here?" Gillette barked.

Lieutenant Geyer put down the shovel and turned slowly. "Helping. I figured there was room for one man."

Gillette glared, furious. "You were supposed to withdraw with the rest of the company."

Geyer's face turned blank with angelic innocence. "I don't like running from a fight. It's unconstitutional," the burly man said dryly. "Besides, I'm tuckered out from too much walking. Figured I'd just rest here a bit."

Gillette frowned his disapproval, but secretly he was grateful to have the big man's support. Geyer was a veteran soldier and a good man to have in a fight.

"You've got shit for brains, Lieutenant."

"Yes, sir," Geyer grinned. "Ain't we all."

*

The Chinese attacked three minutes later.

1st Platoon were spread thinly along the verge of the road, with the M240 in the center of their line. Gillette was crouched in cover close to the machine gun with Lieutenant Geyer and the platoon's leader within shouting distance on either side of him.

"Here they come!" a voice on the left flank of the line cried out.

Gillette looked up and saw movement backlit against the far wall of forest; dozens of Chinese soldiers coming forward through the long grass, darting and jinking between trees as they advanced. They were still several hundred yards away but moving with purposeful determination.

Gillette clapped the machine gun operator on the shoulder. "Open fire," he ordered.

It was long range, but that was the point. Gillette's best hope was to slow down the Chinese attack before it could reach the far side of the road and overwhelm his men. Massed rifle fire from a platoon of troops at close quarters wouldn't be enough to hold back the Chinese attack. He had to fend them off from a distance and pray the Chinese would be forced to caution.

He checked his watch. It had been four minutes since the rest of the battalion had withdrawn towards the Yalu.

The M240 roared into life, bellowing fury and spitting fire. The sound of the machine gun hammered against the trees.

The Chinese infantry reacted intuitively, throwing themselves down in the long grass and scrabbling for cover as a fury of bullets plucked at the air around them. Several of the enemy paused their advance to return fire, aiming wildly. A Chinese officer barked furiously at his men and the line went grudgingly forward once more.

"Keep firing. Keep them pinned down," Gillette told the machine gun crew, then beckoned Lieutenant Geyer to him.

"You wanted to be a part of this shit-fight, so now you're going to earn your keep. Here's what I want you to do," Gillette quickly outlined his plan.

The two officers waited for the M240 to open fire again. As soon as the drumming hammer of the machine gun roared, they broke apart. Geyer ran one hundred yards to the left, doubled over and darting between trees, and Gillette ran to the right, twisting and jinking, ducked low to remain in cover. When he was in position far beyond the end of the American line, he dropped to the ground and heaved in a gasping breath. As soon as the M240 fell silent he scrambled to his knees and cupped his hands around his mouth.

"Battalion! Prepare to open fire!" he cried out, his voice carrying in the sudden eerie stillness of the forest. A moment later he heard Geyer's voice, drifting out of the forest wall two hundred yards away to his left.

"Alpha Company. Prepare to fire mortars!"

Gillette waited for a few pounding seconds and then dashed another twenty paces to his right. "Charlie Company! Bring up the heavy machine guns!"

He fired a spray of gunfire towards the Chinese, not even bothering to aim his M4, then began to work his way back towards 1st Platoon's position. Twice he paused to shout more orders, giving the impression that the enemy were facing a force of at least battalion strength.

Lieutenant Geyer met Gillette behind the M240. Geyer was red-faced and grinning like a wayward schoolboy up to mischief. "Now what?"

Gillette shrugged and then peered hard towards the Chinese. They were advancing in company strength but moving cautiously, being urged on by the demanding barks of their officers.

Gillette checked his watch. Seven minutes had elapsed since the rest of the battalion had begun their retreat towards the Yalu.

"Any moment now, the enemy are going to hit us with smoke and then they'll charge," Gillette said. "We won't be able to hold them. The best we can do is use the next few moments to kill as many of their officers as we can. Who are our best shots?"

Geyer shrugged. "Kelly and Vasquez," he said.

"Okay. Go and find them. Tell them to open fire on any Chinese soldier who looks like an officer."

Geyer went scampering away to find the two riflemen and Gillette turned his attention back to the Chinese. The nearest enemy troops had closed to within a couple of hundred paces of the road. The Chinese infantry were working like skirmishers; darting forward under the watchful cover of their companions to leapfrog their way forward.

A shot rang out from somewhere along the American line to tell Gillette that Kelly and Vasquez had begun their grim work and then the enemy mortars opened fire, straddling the road with a barrage of smoke rounds. The Chinese had the range and the smoke fell in a tight pattern, instantly blanketing the gravel trail in a swirling veil of white-grey clouds.

Gillette barked a tight warning to his men. "Pepper them with the grenade launchers, and then open fire at anything that moves. Keep firing until there's no one left to kill!"

Lieutenant Geyer reappeared at his shoulder. Gillette checked his watch and then seized the lieutenant's shoulder.

"We've got to hold them off for a couple more minutes," he spoke urgently against a sudden soundtrack of grenades exploding in the mid-distance as the men carried out his orders. "When I give you the word, I want you to lead the men back towards the Yalu. The Colonel is commanding a rear guard. Find them and get the boys safely back to camp."

"What about you?" Geyer growled.

"I'm going to stay for as long as the M240 has ammunition. Then I'll follow."

"I'll stay with you," Geyer said firmly.

"No. You're going to lead the men to safety. I'm putting them under your command. I know you'll do a better job than I ever did."

"But –"

"No," Gillette shook his head. "You have your orders, Lieutenant. I expect you to follow them."

The swiftest of the enemy reached the far side of the road, shrouded by the dense blanket of smoke, and then suddenly they emerged through the haze, roaring their war cries and firing wildly into the void. An enemy bullet whizzed an inch past Lieutenant Geyer's face and he fired back instinctively; spraying the greyness directly ahead of him with a short burst of gunfire. Somewhere in the mist an enemy soldier howled in pain and Geyer swore savage triumph.

"Die you fuckers! Die!" he spat, then fired again.

The M240 roared and the rest of the platoon added their weapons to the firefight, blazing at the ghostly grey shapes that burst across the road. A rifleman was struck in the thigh by an errant Chinese bullet and fell back into the long grass, clutching at his wound and grimacing. A man fighting close to Gillette was hit flush in the face. The bullet tore out through the back of the man's skull, dashing splattered bone fragments and gore across the trunk of a nearby tree.

Gillette emptied his magazine into a thicket of grey charging shapes, then reloaded with the deft practiced skill of a veteran and fired again, all the while a clock ticking inside his head, counting down the seconds. An enemy soldier broke through the smoke, charging like a wild bull, his assault rifle held low across his hip. He fired into the tree line and Gillette felt the bullet pluck at the fabric of his uniform sleeve. He swiveled at the hips and fired from close range, knocking the enemy soldier to the ground. The man fell screaming in a gush of bright red blood.

Gillette turned and his desperate eyes hunted the tree line for Lieutenant Geyer.

"Go! Go now!"

Geyer hesitated and Gillette swore.

"First platoon withdraw! Fall back! Fall back!"

That forced the issue and left Geyer with no option. The men scrambled to their feet and began to melt away into the woods, still firing but going backwards. Gillette slung his M4 across his back and then threw himself down behind the abandoned M240. He caught a last fleeting glance of Geyer and barked at him a final time.

"Get the men safely back to the Yalu!"

*

The M240 had a full belt of ammunition loaded; a hundred rounds. Gillette hunkered down behind the weapon and wedged the stock tight into his right shoulder. Lying prone, he squeezed the trigger and fired a short ten-round burst into the smoke. The weapon juddered into his body, sounding like a jackhammer as the spent shell casings were ejected, spinning into the long grass at his side. There was no need to sight a target; the Chinese were a swarm of grey shifting shapes, some as close as thirty paces, some merely dark specters further into the distance. Gillette heard himself growling vengeance as he fired.

An enemy soldier who had paused disoriented in the middle of the road was cut down by the first spray of gunfire; flung backwards, his arms flailing as the rounds punched through his chest. He fell to his knees, but he was already dead. His uniform was a riot of violent bloody splashes; his face in death fixed with an excruciating expression of pain. Gillette paused for a heartbeat and then fired again – another short, sharp burst of drumming gunfire that cut a swathe through the nearest Chinese troops and forced others to throw themselves to the ground and scrabble for cover.

He paused long enough for the echo of the hammering machine gun to fade into the forest, and then squeezed off another burst, this time traversing the weapon as he fired. Three more Chinese soldiers were cut down. One jerked like a puppet on a string and then fell. Another was caught in mid-stride as he gathered himself to cross the road. A hail of bullets battered him over and ripped him to pieces. The third man somehow survived the spitting gunfire. Struck in the leg, he toppled like a tenpin which probably saved his life. He writhed on the ground, screaming a high-pitched wail for help at the men who ran past him heedless of his appeals.

Then the first Chinese hand grenade fell out of the smoky shroud and landed ten yards to the left of Gillette. The grenade exploded in a thunderclap of sound and a flash of searing bright light. Clumps of flung soil landed on Gillette's back and the air around him turned thick with dust. He fired again, sweeping the barrel of the machine gun from left to right, holding the trigger down. His teeth rattled in his head and his vision jumped and blurred. The last rounds in the ammunition belt disappeared into the weapon's breach and then the M240 suddenly stopped firing.

The silence was appalling; a crushing eerie weight fraught with menace. Gillette sprang to his feet. He had done everything he could. Now the only thing left to do was to run like a man with the devil on his heels.

Gillette fled.

In the eerie aftermath after the roar of the M240, the Chinese came through the twisting smoke with creeping wary caution, and it took a full minute before they realized to their astonishment and outrage that the Americans had fled the battlefield. The officer commanding the company snarled like a savage wolf denied its prey. He ordered his men to the pursuit.

Gillette heard the shrill whistles and knew the Chinese were behind him, like beaters driving the game during a hunt. They were moving through the forest in teams, shouting and randomly firing their weapons. He heard a shout and cringed, expecting any moment to be cut down by gunfire. But no shots rang out. He ran on, his heart thumping wildly in his chest.

He leaped a fallen log, landed like a cat and pushed on. His boots felt like lead weights and sweat ran stinging into his eyes. He ran with his body tensed and his jaw clenched and felt a stabbing stitch like a knife in his side. He blundered into a tree and paused for a moment, heaving for breath and doubled over while he searched for signs of his pursuers. He could hear them clearly but could see no signs of the enemy. They were there, somewhere just beyond his vision – maybe a couple of hundred yards behind him. Another whistle sounded shrilly and then a shot rang out, gouging a chunk of bark from the tree Gillette was leaning against.

The bullet had flown high and missed him by at least three feet, but it was enough to startle Gillette. He dashed away, crashing through the undergrowth, his shirt soaked wet with sweat and his legs like rubber beneath him.

Another cry went up from somewhere behind him and Gillette felt himself tense again with a sense of fatal foreboding. He could feel his skin crawling with tiny insects of dread. The cry was taken up by another voice, this one louder, barking orders. Gillette jinked to his left and then a shot rang out through the forest and slammed against Gillette's ears.

A white-hot bolt of savage pain shot through his leg, and he felt himself falling. His right leg went numb and then his knee collapsed under his weight. He went down hard, hitting the forest floor face-first. Then the pain came; a surging wave of agony unlike anything he had ever experienced before. He writhed on the ground, clutching at his knee and felt his fingers awash with warm sticky blood. When he looked down, his pants were soaked red and there were flecks of white jagged bone and cartilage where his kneecap had been.

Gillette swore and screamed in pain, gritting his teeth as wave after wave of black pain washed over him. He felt himself sinking into shock and then, through the crashing torture, he heard a cruel volley of M4 fire.

He fell back, staring up at the canopy of foliage overhead, his eyes beginning to lose focus, his heart still pounding, seeming to match tempo with each fresh stab of pain. Then faces emerged through the blur, crowding around him; American faces. Faces of men he knew.

Colonel Reilly crouched down beside Gillette, his creased with concern.

"You're okay. You're gonna make it," Colonel Reilly said gently. "Just hold tight and let the medics do their work."

*

Gillette came drifting up through the morphine delirium and the closer he rose to the surface of consciousness, the sharper the pain in his leg intensified. He came alert with a start and a groan of agony. His face flushed burning hot and his brow broke out in blisters of perspiration.

He was lying on a stretcher, under a canvas canopy, attached to a drip. In the background, somewhere nearby but out of sight, he could hear the thwacking thump of helicopter rotors beating at the air. Major Guy Yee leaned over Gillette and smiled with kindly benevolence.

"You're back at base, Razor. You're going to be okay. We're medevacking you out to a field hospital and then moving you on to Seoul for surgery on your shattered kneecap," the major explained quickly, then his expression softened into a look of compassion. "Your war is over but you're going home a hero. Colonel Reilly has recommended you for a Silver Star."

Epilogue:
12 months later.

Buck Gillette stepped gingerly over a fallen log under the watchful eyes of his guide, using the walking stick to offset the limping drag of his leg and maintain his balance. His face was tight with strain and dripping from sweaty exertion, his eyes downcast and his Levi's clinging to his legs. Under his t-shirt his body was gaunt and wasted from the long months of rehabilitation so that he looked lanky and haunted as a scarecrow.

He stopped for a moment to draw a deep breath and asked his guide, "How much further?"

"Just another few minutes, good sir," the Chinese woman spoke polite, fluent English. "We are almost at the place."

Gillette nodded, his bony jaw thrust forward, his brow furrowed from the enormity of the effort he had made to complete this sacred pilgrimage; to keep the promise he had made to himself.

"Lead the way," he said softly.

They emerged from the trail onto a gentle rise of ground and for a moment Gillette did not recognize the location. So much that he remembered had changed dramatically in the past year. Now the gentle valley that once held the Chinese comms bunker was re-forested; nature had reclaimed the land.

He saw it then, slowly emerging from within the long grass and the newly-grown saplings. He saw the great gouge in the earth where the bunker buster had exploded, and he saw the heaved piles of earth like the rim of a dormant volcano. Grass and wildflowers now grew amongst the up-churned earth and the broken slabs of concrete.

"My God," he breathed as everything came rushing back to him in vivid snatches and lurid, bloody detail. He propped for a long moment, leaning heavily on the walking stick and let himself re-live the nightmare, as if doing so was a cathartic part of the recovery process. He felt his eyes prickle and burn with emotional tears, but he blinked them away.

"Thank you," he said quietly to his guide. "Please wait here. I will not be long."

He went down the gentle slope slowly, moving like an old man, the stiff drag of his damaged knee forcing him to pause several times. He reached the valley floor with his shoulders hunched and gasping for breath.

He cast his eyes ahead and saw a young tree that had sprouted from the carnage of the vast bomb crater. He hobbled towards it, straightening his back and squaring his shoulders, walking tall. He reached the tree and bowed his head respectfully. From the pocket of his jeans, he retrieved the Silver Star. He laid the medal at the base of the sapling, then stepped back one pace and saluted as the tears finally spilled down his face in a wave of unashamed emotion.

"I award this medal for valor to Lieutenant Michael Loftus and the platoon of 4th Rangers, British Army, who died at this place defending freedom," he spoke solemnly, muttering the private oath of honor. "True heroes all. Brave men who taught me the meaning of duty and sacrifice and respect. May they forever be remembered for their selfless gallantry."

Acknowledgements:

The greatest thrill of writing, for me, is the opportunity to research the subject matter and to work with military, political and historical experts from around the world. I had a lot of help researching this book from the following groups and people. I am forever grateful for their willing enthusiasm and cooperation. Any remaining technical errors are mine.

Jill Blasy:

Jill has the editorial eye of an eagle! I trust Jill to read every manuscript, picking up typographical errors, missing commas, and for her general 'sense' of the book. Jill has been a great friend and a valuable part of my team for several years.

Jan Wade:

Jan is my Personal Assistant and an indispensable part of my team. She is a thoughtful, thorough, professional and persistent pleasure to work with. Chances are, if you're reading this book, it's due to Jan's engaging marketing and promotional efforts.

Dale Simpson:

Dale is a retired Special Forces operator who has been helping me with the military aspects of my writing since I first put pen to paper. He is my first point of contact for military technical advice. Over the years that he has been saving me from stupid mistakes we've become firm friends. The authenticity of the action and combat sequences in this novel are due to Dale's diligence and willing cooperation.

Dion Walker Sr:

Sergeant First Class (Retired) Dion Walker Sr, served 21 proud years in the US Army with deployments during Operation Desert Shield/Storm, Operation Intrinsic Action and Operation Iraqi Freedom. For 17 years he was a tanker in several Armor Battalions and Cavalry Squadrons before spending 4 years as an MGS (Stryker Mobile Gun System) Platoon Sergeant in a Stryker Infantry Company.

Website: https://www.worldwar3timeline.com

Printed in Great Britain
by Amazon